DESERT ROSE

K. MOORE

ISBN-13: 978-1-7328844-0-3

PREFACE

———

Once upon a time, a mythical land sparkled in the sunlight, its inhabitants truly mesmerizing. The women were reputed to be the most beautiful in the world. They wore willowy skirts sewn from fine silks that made any movement appear like a seductive dance and tight-fitted blouses covered in gems that barely hid their breasts. Faces, adorned with metallic masks, revealed only dark eyes lined in kohl and luscious red-stained lips, hinting at the beauty hidden beneath.

The men were equally majestic, wearing flowing cotton *thobes* with their *jambiyya* attached around their waists. Welcoming smiles lit their faces while they watched the *dhows* sail in from Persia, piled high with carpets, gold, spices from the Orient, exotic trinkets in all forms, and on the rare occasion … women.

In full view of the masses, merchants and their customers would sit on ornate-colored cushions, deep in discussion while drinking sweet tea and sharing the *shisha* pipe as they waited for the goods to be unloaded at the port in Dubai Creek.

The *dhows*, mostly commanded by sailors from the subcontinent, stood ready to barter their wares, trading for the most beautiful and precious export of the area—pearls.

As time went by, the value of natural pearls crashed due to the influx of Japanese cultured pearls, causing the regional economy to collapse. Years passed as the Emirati people tried to find their place in the new world. During this time, as the region continued to adapt to the increasingly shifting economic environment and became influenced by regional and global politics, technology, and newly built infrastructure, the culture slowly changed. The carefree life of the Arabian Gulf, the nomadic *bedu*, was soon forgotten, only to be replaced by Western greed.

The imagery of what once was is but a myth. Tall tales were told under the starry sky on the non-magic carpet as the cool breeze allowed the sand to sway to its music. Tales told of a land mixed with intrigue and adventure that never really existed.

But tales are only fabled stories. Fairy tales mixed with a hint of truth. The colorful representation painting a pretty picture, for there was only ever the hardship and brutality of human existence.

There is no happily ever after.

The Arabian Tales never existed.

It is all just a lie.

PART 1

I

———

I love summer. Not the Dubai summer with its scorching heat, but the time the kids and I spend sans the normal routine of school and sporting activities. I also love spending time away from Dubai, back in the US. What I don't enjoy so much is coming home.

Home.

Funny how you get used to a state of being where the unusual and abnormal become the norm. When did living in a beige villa in a beige suburb in the middle of the beige desert become normal? But it gets to the point where it's the norm, and all the bad that comes along with the good is considered just that—normal. From the dust-encrusted streets sweltering in the heat and humidity to the shiny polish of the air-conditioned malls. Children are not playing in the streets on bikes or scooters but wandering the malls with pockets filled with cash and multiple Apple devices.

Sometimes, I worry how this environment, this constant state of bling, will affect my kids. They're growing up in a culturally diverse environment, and they are acutely aware of the class system and where they fit into it. A class system no one overtly talks about, or if they do, it's guffawed over while drinking wine in some elitist bar. A system discussed by the uniformed maids or *shalwar kameez*–cloaked gardeners as they loiter at the small shops by the mosques. The divide between the *us* and *them* is so big, no skilled engineer would be able to design a bridge between the two worlds.

Thing is, the money's good. The schools are good. And, if we're really going to admit to social crimes, having a maid and gardener is freeing. It allows the time to focus on what's important.

Who am I kidding? Not having to do washing or ironing, cleaning or cooking is pretty special. It's great up to the point when your maid is still on leave and someone else has to do the household chores. Or the grocery shopping. Or the childminding.

But even having a maid doesn't get you out of doing some of the shopping, which is why we're still in the Mall of the Emirates half an hour before *iftar*—the breaking of the Ramadan fast.

With cool air blowing from the vents above, I'm flustered and uncomfortably cold as the perspiration gained from spending five minutes outside cools, starching the salt in my clothes. Thankfully, the store's not very busy. Shoppers are mainly of the South Asian working class, judging by their attire. No Western expats from what I can see. No, they'd be as far away from this madness as possible.

"Goldfish? Who said Carrefour had Goldfish crackers? Stupid ExpatWomen's forum," I mumble to myself while scanning the shelves.

Sarah and Liam are dragging their feet somewhere behind me as I try to navigate the aisles as quickly as I can.

"Come on, kids. Let's go."

The cart rumbles forward, clinking as the dented wheel throws off the balance for each revolution. The aisles are a confusing mass of rainbow colors, products uniformly lined up shelf after shelf. Like many grocery stores in Dubai, Carrefour carries goods from countries represented by its varied expat community. This just adds to the confusion for shoppers and store stackers alike with products placed in the most bizarre places. I'm sure this is what's happened with the Goldfish. I should just give up and come back in a week after a conscientious expat updates the forum as to the exact location for them.

Carrefour is a French chain store, similar to Walmart but with a bit more style, given its origins. While many of the South Asians shop at Carrefour for the cheap prices, most of the expats only venture in once a month to stock up on bulk items or cleaning supplies. The bakery and fresh produce vary in quality.

Unlike the warehouse style of Costco, Carrefour is just a grocery store.

"Stay with me, kids. I don't want to chase you all over the store." I come to a halt and pull out my cell phone to check the digital clock. It's time to go. Way past time to go.

"This sucks. Can't we meet you at Magic Planet?" Liam says as he falls in behind me, referring to the kids arcade and play area that takes up almost an entire level next to the indoor ski slope.

"No, we need to go," I say absently as my fingers make quick work of typing out a message to our housemaid, Anika, asking her to prepare dinner. As it is, we still need to check out and load the car. It's not going to happen before *iftar*, and we're going to get stuck in traffic.

Pocketing my phone, I turn toward my son and search over his shoulder, back up the aisle. "Where's Sarah?"

"I don't know. She was just here," he answers, unperturbed, following my gaze. "She said she wanted some Oreos. Maybe she went to grab a packet."

"Can you go get her, please? We really need to go." I rub my forehead. A headache is forming behind my eyes, the pulse throbbing in my temples. The change in time zones isn't helping at all. Not for the first time, I miss the ease of the small grocery store in Chesapeake.

Liam shuffles off and disappears behind a shelf stacked with rice as I take the time to study the outstanding items on my shopping list. It would be great if I could tick them all off, but I'm not feeling it.

A moment later, Liam reappears with a packet of Oreos. "Nope, she wasn't there."

Great.

"I'm going to kill her. I bet she's over in the toy section." Frustrated and borderline annoyed, I spin the shopping cart around and make my way toward the toys.

I shouldn't have come here today, especially with the kids. What was I thinking?

The cart creaks and rattles as we move to the center corridor dividing the store in two. The place is slowly starting to fill, the area with the premade meals and snacks being the main focus of the crowd. South Asian workers who can't afford extravagant *iftar* dinners held at the upmarket hotels. Workers who seek solace among a group of strangers rather than in their cramped accommodations they probably share with ten others. A group of Indians in moderate office attire who congregate around the electronic section as they patiently count down the time for the *iftar* daily sale to kick off.

The increasing crowd is one of the things I wanted to avoid. My annoyance at Sarah builds as I scan the store, looking for her.

"Sarah?" I call out, ignoring the stares. "Sarah!"

I don't see any sign of her. I push the cart to the side of the aisle and stand on it, gaining a precious few inches of height to look back the way we came. An ache forms in the back of my throat when I fail to see my daughter's golden ponytail.

Where is she?

I waste a few precious moments checking both directions again. Nothing.

I buttonhole a staff member who's busy restocking a shelf with toys. "Excuse me, I'm looking for my daughter. Have you seen a girl with blonde hair?"

"No, madam."

"Are you sure? She would've been just over here, looking at the toys and stickers." My hand grips my churning stomach as my breath comes short and fast. I look around, frantically searching for the telltale flash of her blonde hair.

"No, madam," the worker says, standing and shaking his head. "I have seen no children here in the last thirty minutes."

"Are you sure?" My heart's beating too fast, as though I sprinted five miles uphill instead of having pushed the cart a few hundred feet. A feeling of unease settles over me. "Have you been here the whole time?"

"Yes, madam," he says, nodding. "My manager, he has asked of me to restock all of these small girl dolls. As you can see, I have almost finished from all of these empty boxes, madam."

I stare at the empty boxes, unable to work out what he's trying to say. Ignoring him and his boxes, I turn to Liam.

"Liam, run back to where we were and see if she's there. Maybe she doubled back and we missed her. I'm going to stand over there where I can watch you and keep an eye on the aisles." I motion to a crossroad in the center of the store. It has a clear view of the checkouts, store entrance, and the aisles, acting as the feeder carriageway between all the sections.

As Liam races off, I mark his progress while scanning the store for a blonde ponytail. I swear, if Sarah's left the store to go to Magic Planet, I will kill her. The store continues to fill, marking the end of Ramadan.

Chills that have nothing to do with the air conditioner run down my spine, and my chest tightens when Liam comes running back, shaking his head. A sense of dread slowly creeps over my body. I abandon the shopping cart, grab Liam's arm, and start running through the store.

"Sarah!" I scream, ignoring the looks sent my way.

No. Where is she?

"Sarah!"

Oh God, no, no! Where is she?

"Sarah!"

Liam and I skid to a halt in front of the security guard at the entrance, who looks at us in confusion. My eyes watering, pulse racing, I make an effort to calm down by taking a deep, measured breath.

Swallowing rapidly, I frantically question the guard, "Have you seen a little girl, blonde hair … white hair? She's this tall." I gesture with my hands, showing Sarah's height. "She would've passed through here five, maybe ten minutes ago? Have you seen her?"

"Slow down, madam. What are you looking for?" he asks, looking between me and Liam, eyebrows narrowing slightly.

"Not a what, idiot. A who. I'm looking for my daughter. Have you seen my daughter?" I speak with forced restraint, my voice raised, muscles stiffening.

"No, madam. What does she look like?" He shakes his head, and I curse under my breath at the language barrier.

"She is this tall," I say slowly after taking a deep breath to curb my frustration and increasing anxiety. "She has blonde … or white hair. She was wearing a blue dress."

"About ten years old, madam? In a blue dress with white material on the sleeve and at the bottom?"

I almost faint with relief at his words. *That's Sarah. Thank goodness. He's seen her.*

"Yes! Where is she?"

"It is okay, madam. She left with her Filipino nanny. I am sure that you can call her or meet up with her after you finish the shopping, madam."

"Nanny? What nanny?" I question, eyes blinking rapidly, trying to understand what he's trying to say. "Our housemaid is from Ethiopia, not the Philippines."

Who the hell did she leave with? Where are they?

I stand completely still and close my eyes as my life, my world, flashes before me. My blood turns to ice, and my breath hitches at the end of the increased ragged inhale. Trembling hands clasp in front of my stomach as my body rocks slightly.

Dread, the feeling I was momentarily keeping at bay, returns in full force. I'm in a void of nothingness that constricts my entire being. Opening my eyes, I flinch and stumble as the overly bright fluorescent lighting blinds me. I struggle to inhale as my body becomes weightless, and everything turns black.

2

———

"Madam? Madam?"

"Mom, wake up. Mom!"

"Madam?"

"Dad? It's Liam. There's something wrong with Mom, and we can't find Sarah. No, I called Anika, and she's not at home either."

"Madam?"

"At Carrefour, at the mall."

Liam? Where am I?

My body is heavy. It hurts to move.

I ... I need to be doing something. What's he saying?

White noise is distorting his words.

"Mom?"

Liam?

Oh no, Sarah!

A piercing pain forces me to slowly open my eyes. My fingertips gingerly touch the knot forming on my forehead. "My head."

"Yes, madam, you hit your head when you fainted," a man in a suit standing over me says. He moves like quicksilver, carefully placing a hand on my shoulder to stop me from sitting up. "No, madam. Just one moment. The emergency staff will be here to check you are okay."

My head throbs, and I close my eyes to escape the bright lights. After a moment, I reopen them to look around. A large crowd surrounds us. A few of the young men are taking photos with their cell phones. I cringe and am thankful a uniformed police officer forces them to disperse as the medic team pushes through the crowd toward me.

"Okay, madam, how are you feeling?" the medic asks as he kneels next to me, looking me over. He raises a gloved hand to press against my forehead.

"That hurts," I say, wincing. "I'm okay. Wh-what happened? I need to find my daughter, Sarah—"

"Not until I have cleared you, madam. You have a nasty bump to your head." He holds up the swab marked with crimson. "See the blood? You must have caught the corner of the table as you went down. We must check you over before we can release you."

"No." I pull away from him and shake my head, ignoring the pain. *No time.* "You don't understand. I need to find my daughter …"

The medic looks me over and gently holds me in place. "Yes, so we have heard. The staff here said she left with your nanny. You can see her as soon as I patch you up."

"No … no. My nanny is at the villa. She wouldn't have left. She doesn't know we're here. Sarah wouldn't have left with anyone."

"Okay, madam. The police are here. You can talk to them about it."

"How long was I out for?"

"About ten minutes, maybe more? You took a nasty bump on your way down. And, trust me, that was plenty of time for the chaos, which you see now, to evolve. The poor store security man thinks he is going to lose his job."

"And so he bloody well should if he allowed my child to leave with a stranger!" I snap.

A man in the suit is watching the police deal with the crowd while subtly following the conversation between the medic and me.

He steps toward us and crouches next to the medic. "If it is safe for her to move, can we please take this back to the security office over there?" he says.

The medic helps me stand and ushers Liam to grab my bag. My head hurts with the increasing pressure beneath the skin.

"It might look worse than it actually is," the medic says kindly. "There was a bit of blood that had everyone worried, but the cut is shallow and not very big. No stitches required and nothing a plaster cannot fix. You will need to ice the area though if you want to minimize the swelling and to help the bruising come out."

Trying to blink out the bright spots in my vision resulting from staring into the fluorescent lighting, I grimace at the medic. "*Shukran.* Thank you for your help." My head throbs, and I take a deep breath to help me focus.

Sarah!

I need to find my daughter.

3

———

I struggle to my feet. My stomach becomes weightless, like the bottom has fallen out from under me. My vision blurs. I fight the nausea and turn to the suited man. "Are you in charge here? Please help me find my daughter."

"Yes, ma'am. My name is Abdul Kareem. If we go to my office, I will be able to assist you." He opens his arms, indicating an area behind the security desk.

I grab Liam's hand. He stands tall, closing in, adding support to my shaking frame.

"I called Dad. He's on his way," he whispers as we make our way to what appears to be the Carrefour security room. He reaches up and wipes away the tears that I didn't even notice falling on my face.

My mind replays the last five minutes. No, fifteen, if the medic was correct in saying I was unconscious for ten. Sarah has been missing for ten extra minutes.

"Thanks, Liam. Sorry if I scared you."

"No, Mom, you're fine. I'm worried about Sarah though. They think she left the store with some people. Why would she do that?"

I look at the entourage hovering around us, ushering us toward the office door. They all appear serious, and I catch what could be a concerned glance shared between Abdul Kareem and the policeman who has joined us.

"I'm not sure. None of this makes sense. Did your dad say how long he'd be?"

"He's in Media City. He'll be straight over."

Wincing from the pain, I nod and deliberately blow the air from my lungs as I allow my stiff shoulders to soften. "Good."

Media City is only five minutes away. Looking at the policeman following us into the security room, I'm hoping it doesn't take Kevin much longer than that to get here, as my experience dealing with United Arab Emirate, UAE, officials hasn't been good. Something to do with my status as an expat wife. An American expat wife at that. I'm thankful Liam is by my side. Despite the fact that he's only twelve, having a male family member with me will help them take me seriously.

We crowd into the small room, and what I see takes my breath away. It's a security tech world I wouldn't have anticipated for a mall. Screens line the walls, showing different aspects of the large shopping center but mainly concentrating on the entrances and exits and the areas where the large walkways meet the escalators and lifts. I count five workstations set up under the screens with blinking lights and buttons. It looks like something out of the NASA launch room.

"Wow," Liam says, letting go of my hand and looking around in amazement.

"Yeah, wow," I add.

The setup is something you'd expect from a government or defense building, definitely not a mall.

"Please, Mrs. Johnson, madam, take a seat," Abdul Kareem says, indicating that Liam and I should take one of the desk chairs. "As you can see, this is the central security room for the entire Mall of the Emirates. We are housed down here, adjacent to Carrefour, but we are not part of it.

The Carrefour staff has informed us that you believe your daughter was taken from the store. Is this correct?"

"I-I believe so," I quietly say. The fear that preempted my fainting episode churns my stomach, and its contents threaten to rise. I take a few deep breaths to get it under control before I can continue. "We were shopping. Sarah was there one minute and … gone the next. We searched the store but couldn't find her. The security guard at the main entrance said he saw a girl leaving with someone. I'm not sure what happened after that. I think I fainted."

"Mrs. Johnson, can you describe your daughter to us, please?" Abdul Kareem asks as he motions for his offsider to take notes.

He glances at the policeman and tilts his head to the side, as though seeking permission to continue his line of inquiry. The room becomes even quieter as we look toward the uniformed policeman. Leaning back against the wall, he just nods.

"If you please, Mrs. Johnson."

I clench my hands into fists. One of my nails is chipped. *Why am I noticing this? God, this isn't the time for trivial nonsense.* I briefly close my eyes to take another deep breath. *How can they be so calm? My daughter's missing.*

"Her name is Sarah. She's ten years old. She has blonde hair …"

I watch as the man I assume to be Abdul Kareem's assistant writes something down on a notepad.

"White hair," I add for his benefit. "Her hair is shoulder-length, and it's pulled up in a ponytail. She's wearing a blue dress with white bits of lace on the sleeves and around the neckline. She's about this tall," I add, indicating with my hand a height of approximately fifty-four inches.

Abdul Kareem nods to his assistant. Looking over to us and then to the policeman, the assistant goes to the workstation adjacent to the one where Liam and I are sitting. He inserts some commands and pushes a button, switching off the screen on the wall above him. A few more swipes of the keyboard, and the screens show images of the Carrefour main entrance. Watching, we observe people coming in and out. A flash of blue catches my attention.

"Oh my God! Sarah!" I cry, watching my daughter exit the shop with a short Asian lady dressed in a maid's uniform. I find myself standing, looking at the paused image in horror. That's *my* Sarah leaving the store. *Who the hell is that person holding her hand?* I drop into my seat, sobbing again, but I'm unable to take my eyes from the screen.

"Mrs. Johnson, madam, is that your daughter?" Abdul Kareem asks.

Through tear-soaked eyes, choking back a sob, I bob my head. "Yes," I manage to croak.

Abdul Kareem nods once. His demeanor doesn't change as he looks at the policeman, who has remained silent. They appear calm and resigned, as though this was an expected conclusion.

"What's going on?" I plead, looking between them, the dread overwhelming.

The longer their silence fills the crowded room, the more I can hear my own heartbeat echoing off the tight walls. They are closing in, suffocating my sanity.

The policeman kicks off from the wall and repositions himself in front of the door. "Hello, madam. I am *Mulazim* Ahmed. I think we will wait until your husband gets here before we continue, yes?" His accent is heavy, his words and demeanor dismissive.

I blink once. *Mulazim* is Arabic for lieutenant. *Why is a lieutenant on duty in the mall—and during Ramadan?* The rank sounds too high and important for the position of a glorified mall cop. I'm not complaining. Maybe *he's* the person who can help.

I slightly incline my head to show him I heard his words, frustrated we'll waste more precious moments. The proof of my daughter's abduction is screaming at us from the still on the screen, but we'll wait. Wait for the man of the family to progress the investigation.

"Yes, sir. He shouldn't be too long."

I look down to Liam and squeeze his hand in reassurance. This must be completely daunting for him. He squeezes back, letting me know he's there, not because he's all right. I don't expect him to be all right, and he definitely doesn't look it. I'm sure that the fear and worry I see on his face are reflected on mine—skin drained of color and eyes wide in shock, darting around the room and back down again.

"Dad should be here soon," he whispers, ever the boy emulating a man.

We wait, and even though I want to jump up and down and scream at these people to stop wasting time and do something to find my daughter, to use this fancy surveillance system to work out where she was taken, I don't. It'll do no good. These people treat women as inconsequential.

I sit, trying to portray an outward look of calm and patience, and wait. I'm not calm though. I'm anything but calm. There's nothing I can do because if the lieutenant has told us to wait, then that is what we will do, and no arguing, screaming, crying, or reasoning will get him to change his mind.

As the minutes tick by, I curse this place where we live. I curse the system. The police. The country. The religion. I curse the place forcing me to sit here, treating me like a second-class citizen because of my sex and my citizenship. I try not to imagine where Sarah is and what's happening to her, but I can't help it.

Is she struggling? Is she fighting her abductors? Crying? Screaming? What are they doing with her?

Movement by the door forces my attention away from my daughter's plight and back to the room. As Abdul

Kareem unlocks the door, I glance to the adjacent small security screen.

Kevin.

Thank goodness he's finally here and we can get on with finding Sarah.

4

———

In a matter of seconds, I'm enclosed in Kevin's warm embrace. His button-down work shirt sticks to my face as it soaks up my tears. Strong arms envelop me as I osmotically pass all the responsibility, my stress, and my anxiety over to him. He's experienced in negotiating and dealing with various cultural authorities in his role with the commodity trading company he works for.

"It's going to be okay," he whispers to me. Quickly pressing his lips to my forehead, he turns to the other men. "*Salaamu aleikom, Mulazim. Ismi* Kevin Johnson, *'ana zawje* Jennifer *wa* Liam *'ibni,*" Kevin says as he disengages from me and moves toward Abdul Kareem and Lieutenant Ahmed.

As they shake hands, the required pleasantries and introductions are complete.

"Please take a seat, Mr. Johnson," Lieutenant Ahmed says, indicating the chair adjacent to mine.

We all sit before he continues.

"I work for the assistant director for Offender Follow-Up and Foreigners. We have both an investigation department and a control border access department. Your wife, Mrs. Johnson, has alleged that your daughter went missing from Carrefour—"

"She was taken. We saw it on the security footage!" I indignantly interrupt.

Kevin places a hand on my arm, silently asking me to calm down and be quiet. It's okay for him; he's used to the cultural foreplay and wading through the political quagmire. Me, not so much. I want to scream at these guys, tell them to get on with it. We are wasting precious time, sitting around, doing nothing. For all we know, Sarah could have crossed the border by now.

The lieutenant frowns at the interruption. Looking at me, he nods. "Yes, we have seen a person, who your wife could not identify, leaving the shop with your daughter. She appears to be Filipino and was dressed in a housemaid's uniform. We were able to track them through the mall's security camera network and observed them meeting a male before departing the vicinity of the mall. We have the make and model of the car they were driving, and our mobile police unit has been briefed, as have the officers working on the border gates."

Staring at the lieutenant, I take in all of this information. There was no indication he did anything but wait for my husband to arrive. On one hand, the withheld information annoys me. But at least they're taking this seriously. To know they started investigating and were able to track Sarah's movements is both a relief and devastation.

"Oh my gosh," I whisper to Kevin.

Without taking his eyes from the lieutenant, he squeezes my hand in response.

"So, I take it, you've started an active investigation to find my daughter?" he asks.

"Yes, sir," Abdul Kareem answers. "We began tracking your daughter through the footage as soon as we identified her. The police have been on high alert and looking ever since."

"Why ..." Kevin starts, letting go of my hand and gesturing around the room toward the various monitors and screens. "Why do you have all of this here, in the Mall of the Emirates?"

"Mr. Johnson, what we have and do not have in this place is of no concern to you or your wife," Lieutenant Ahmed answers. "What is of concern is that we were able to identify your daughter, and we are taking every step possible to locate her."

"Okay. So, what do we do now?"

"Nothing. There is nothing for you to do. I suggest that you go back to your home. We will keep you up-to-date with the investigation." As though his words are the final ones to be said on the matter, Lieutenant Ahmed nods to us, turns, and exits the room in three short steps.

Kevin repeats his question, this time directing it to Abdul Kareem. "What can we do now?"

"Nothing, sir. As the lieutenant said, there is nothing you can do but wait. I only look after the security for the mall, and I cannot provide you with any further information than that which has already been shared."

"Can we get a copy of the still image of the person who took Sarah?" Kevin asks, gesturing to one of the monitors above us.

The question hangs in the air as Abdul Kareem takes the time to consider it. A frown crosses his face, and after what's clearly an internal debate, he slowly nods.

"I don't think it would be a problem. I should probably check with Lieutenant Ahmed, but I am sure it will be okay. Just give me a few minutes to organize it."

The door closes behind him, and I turn to Kevin. "Kevin, I …"

"Not now, Jen. Wait until we have some privacy." He subtly nods to a camera located in the corner of the room.

Another camera. If it isn't enough for us to find out they have the entire mall under surveillance, they're also watching the watchers.

I take his hand and hold on as though death were trying to tear us apart, my knuckles white. We sit and wait.

After a few minutes, both the lieutenant and Abdul Kareem return, speaking softly to each other. The words, not quite loud enough for us to catch, are in Arabic. The lieutenant shakes his head in exasperation before glowering at us. With a final nod to Abdul Kareem, he exits the room again.

Abdul Kareem offers us an apologetic smile and raises his index finger for us to wait another moment. He moves to the operator at the far workstation and talks to him in Arabic.

A call comes in for Kevin on his cell. He steps out to take it, brushing by the two men as he does. I watch him go, wondering what's more important than being in here with Liam and me.

5

———

Time passing slowly is such a cliché. The clock's second hand is nothing but an erratic heartbeat, speeding up with the chaos of time running away. Every passing minute is another minute Sarah's been missing. The more minutes that pass, the harder it will be to find her. Every second counts. I want the second hand to slow down to give time for the authorities to find her. To find her before ...

I don't even want to think about what could come next. Still images of every child abduction or horror movie flick through my mind. My head is throbbing. My heart is hurting, aching. Someone has thrust their hand through my chest and is squeezing my heart, but it's not exploding; it's slowly crumbling.

"Jen, I think it's time for you and Liam to head on home. There's nothing more you can do here now," Kevin says, having reentered the room, pulling me out of my morbid thoughts. "I've called Jacquie. She's on her way to pick you up, and she will stay with you until I get back. I still need to meet with the US Embassy staff after I finish up here."

I look at him in confusion, wondering why I'm being sidelined. And why he called Jacquie and not one of my friends, like Melanie. Or even Kate or Monica, whose husbands work with Kevin and kids go to school with ours. Jacquie's a work colleague of Kevin's, a lawyer. She and I don't socialize. He has a point though. Liam shouldn't be here to see this. He should be home, secure behind the walls of our villa.

"Okay," I say, surprised at how meek it sounds.

He reaches down and pulls me up into his arms, hugging me before placing a chaste kiss on my forehead. Gently pulling away, he looks me in the eyes. "It's going to be all right, Jen. The police will find her. Let's trust in the process. In the meantime, you and Liam need to go home and get some rest." He briefly glances down at his phone as it vibrates, nodding to himself once before looking up. "Jacquie's outside at the ground-floor parking entrance. You should get going, okay?"

"Okay."

"Jen," he says, bringing my eyes back to him, "we will find her."

I nod and grab Liam's hand. "Come on, kid. Let's go home. Dad's here now. He'll make sure they find Sarah."

Lieutenant Ahmed and Abdul Kareem are in the corner, talking quietly. Lost in my thoughts, I missed the lieutenant's return. I head in their direction, and when the lieutenant sees me, he cuts short their conversation.

"Excuse me, Lieutenant, Abdul Kareem."

"Yes, Mrs. Johnson." The lieutenant's reply is curt. He stands tall and regards me with an air of disdain.

With a deep breath, I turn to Abdul Kareem. "Thank you. Thank you for being there after my fainting episode and initiating the response and search so quickly. If you weren't there, I'm not too sure what I would've done."

"You are most welcome, Mrs. Johnson. I am glad to see you are feeling a little better. I'll have someone escort you to your car."

The lieutenant frowns. "Mrs. Johnson, your husband is here now. We will deal with him directly, regarding the search for your daughter."

Annoyed at the obvious dismissal but too emotionally exhausted to really give a shit about it, I nod to convey my reluctant understanding. My head throbs at the action. "Thank you, Lieutenant, Abdul Kareem. Good evening, gentlemen."

Shuffling along with Liam toward the door, I take another look at the room. Kevin has his back to us, talking animatedly on his cell phone. Thankful he's here to navigate the cultural minefield and deal with the authorities, I close my eyes and take another deep breath before exiting the room.

Leaving behind the quiet of the security room throws us into the full din of the mall. People are everywhere, wandering in and out of shops, bags in hand. The noise and bright lights are enough to momentarily make me lose my step. I pull Liam closer to me as my senses adjust.

Negotiating the crowds is nothing short of frustrating. The Carrefour entrance is almost shoulder-to-shoulder with bodies. *Iftar* has passed, and the mall has definitely filled in its wake. Unwashed bodies mix with the perfectly coiffed, and the sickly sweet stench of body odor with a Dior aftertaste wafts freely. It takes effort and concentration for me to place one foot in front of the other and drive forward.

As we exit the mall into the ground floor parking area, I almost cry in relief at a much-needed familiar face. Jacquie's waiting by her Bugatti, and she comes rushing, pulling us both into a hug.

"Jen, I'm so sorry," she whispers.

Jacquie herds us toward the car, my legs on autopilot as I try to ignore the crowd's inquisitive looks. Red and sleek, the Bugatti's her pride and joy, a gift from one of her Saudi clients, and it always brings attention. Sarah's ridden in the car a few times. She enjoyed it. Right now, I couldn't care less about Jacquie's car. I want my daughter. To brush her hair. To fix her favorite dinner.

"When Kevin called ... I just can't imagine. Don't worry, babe; between him, the embassy, and the authorities, they *will* get her back."

Before I realize it, we are in the car, exiting the lot, and heading toward Sheikh Zayed Road. We switch lanes and slow to a crawl as cars back up before the Umm Suqeim Street turnoff. The silence within the car doesn't reflect the chaos of the evening traffic, nor does it reflect the acid churning in my stomach.

"Stupid roadworks ... stupid Ramadan," Jacquie mumbles as she negotiates her way left to merge into the so-called fast lane. Weaving through the traffic, she gets us to the interchange that will lead into our Jumeirah neighborhood.

Jacquie pulls in front of my villa and places the car in park, leaving the engine running. She looks at my still body and gently grasps my hand. "Let's get inside, Jen."

Unclasping my seat belt, I sit, stunned, momentarily wondering how I fastened it in the first place. My head is throbbing, and the nausea threatens to overwhelm me. Perhaps I have a concussion. As I feel a squeeze on my hand, I blink slowly and look up. I wonder why the surreal view of Ramadan dusk grabs my attention. The crescent moon is high in the sky. Although the sun is no longer shining, stifling heat rises from the bitumen road.

I climb out of the vehicle, and the humidity clings to me, adding extra weight to my already drained body. I concentrate on putting one foot in front of the other. *When has walking ever required such attention or been so difficult?*

Liam and Jacquie are waiting for me at the front door.

How did we get here? Shaking off the dizziness, I unlock it and enter, welcoming the air-conditioned interior.

Jacquie takes charge. "Liam, how about you head on up and grab a quick shower? I'll look after your mom and see if we can rustle up some food."

"Okay. When do you think they'll bring Sarah home?" he asks.

"Hopefully soon, baby."

I start at the term of endearment used while she pulls him into a hug before I freeze. It's a familiar scene from only a few days ago. Sarah hugged her when our paths accidentally crossed at the Dallas airport as she was readying to board with the other first-class passengers. The people Jacquie were traveling with all stopped to smile and say their hellos to Sarah. I blink away the image.

With Liam out of the picture, Jacquie takes me by the arm and leads me into the kitchen. I collapse onto one of the cane kitchen bench chairs and look at her in desperation.

"Why …" I start before a sob chokes me. After a deep breath, I try again. "How did this happen, Jacquie? How could this have happened?"

Before she can respond, the kitchen door opens, and our housemaid enters with a dishcloth in her hand. She takes one look at me and stiffens. The door slams behind her, and she wrings the cloth between her hands.

"Madam? Madam? What is happening?"

"Anika!" I wrap the lady in my arms as the tears continue to fall. "Sarah was kidnapped from the mall." I sob, pulling away from her.

"No. No, madam, no!" Anika says, eyes wide with shock. "This is not good, madam. Do you know what will happen to her? In Ethiopia, nothing good comes to girls who are stolen from their families."

"Anika!" Jacquie shouts before I can reply. "Please, enough of that! Liam is upstairs in the shower. Prepare him some food and keep an eye on him, please. I'll take madam into the back room to rest. I'll let you know if we need anything."

Jacquie walks me to the rear sitting room adjacent to the pool. As an afterthought, she turns back toward the maid. "Anika, the police are investigating Sarah's disappearance. You are *not* to talk to anyone other than sir or madam regarding this. No gossiping to your maid friends. No one. Are we understood?"

"Yes, madam." Anika's eyes lower in submission, and her shoulders hunch forward.

"Good."

I should feel bad about the way Jacquie dressed down Anika and issued her orders, but my mind barely registers it. Anika is frantic. I saw it in her eyes before she was put in her place. I can't console her now. I don't have the energy for dealing with anyone else's fear, except my own.

After the double doors to the sitting room slam shut, Jacquie grabs two tumblers and a bottle of whisky from the armoire. With a flick of a switch, the pool illuminates the outdoor garden area. I collapse into the nearest chair, the plush couch next to me. Jacquie pours two stiff drinks.

"Here," she says.

Taking a sip and sitting back, I lose myself to the smell of the hard liquor. Slightly floral with a hint of honey, the smell converts to flavor as it meets my tongue. I close my eyes and savor the initial burn as it works its way down my throat. My taste buds adapt with the second sip. Whisky is magic, purposefully moving through the body, looking to infiltrate all nerve endings to brainwash them into weightlessness.

My hand clenches into a fist and then opens, palm facing down. Looking at it, I repeat the motion. The whisky has reached my fingers, and I smile at the sensation.

"Do you need to talk about it?" Jacquie asks hesitantly, shuffling uncomfortably in her seat.

I like that. I like that she doesn't demand I talk, nor does she ask if I want to talk. I don't want to talk at all.

My mind feels as though it's wading through some clouds, the suction from them making it difficult to move and to breathe. These aren't fluffy white clouds, all light and pretty. These are dense and dark, much like the storm clouds over a Virginia winter. Above the clouds, sunshine and blue sky continue into forever. Peaceful. Serene. Below, however, is a turmoil of darkness with wind, rain, and the occasional thunderclap after a lightning strike. I'm being sucked down, sinking into them, as though into quicksand. My body is singed from the lightning strike that is becoming my living nightmare.

I sit up and open my eyes. "I'm not sure what to say, Jacquie. I'm just so fucking scared. What if they can't find her?"

"They'll find her."

"But what if they can't? What if something happens ..."

"Jen, you can't think like that. You have to stay positive. Stay strong. You have to stay strong for Sarah and Liam."

"I know. I just feel so stupid. Why was I at Carrefour anyway? Why was I rushing around, trying to get everything and fit everything in? What was the rush?"

"You were doing what you do. There's no right or wrong time to go to the store."

"No, but I didn't *need* to go right then. I didn't *need* to try to fit it in then. Everyone knows the best time to go is at opening. Not in the fucking afternoon just before *iftar* during fucking Ramadan with the fucking children!"

Gulping down the remaining whisky, I sit back again, eyes closed. My head rests back onto the top of the lounge, and I exhale the spirit's fumes. Swallowing back a sob, I tightly squeeze my eyes shut until I can see nothing but white spots on my lids.

"Jen, look at me."

I open my eyes.

"They. Will. Find. Her."

6

———

Those four words echo through my mind.

"They. Will. Find. Her."

No four words have ever been truer. No four words have ever meant so much.

Jacquie's voice knocks me from my stupor. "Why don't you tell me what happened? I only know what Kevin told me over the phone. That Sarah was taken. Has she been kidnapped?"

Concern is etched on Jacquie's face as she takes a sip of her drink, her eyes never leaving mine. I find it weird that she's here with me but strangely comforting.

"We were in Carrefour. I can't even remember what we were looking for. We were doing a quick shop, trying to get in and out before *iftar* to miss all of the traffic and chaos. She … she … she was there one minute, and then she wasn't."

Jacquie grabs the whisky from the armoire. Her slender hand wraps around the bottle as she sits back down and pours us another generous drink. I tell her what happened in every tiny detail, up to the point where I fainted, reliving the horror.

Jacquie stops still. "You hit your head?"

"Yes." I grimace, gently touching the bandage on my head. Even in panic-ridden grief, I can't contain my sarcasm. "This bandage is not a fashion accessory. Trust me on that."

"Do you have a headache? Do you need any Tylenol or Advil?"

"No, no. They gave me something for that. The whisky's doing the rest." I pray it will start working soon, as my pulse is vibrating across my forehead, between my temples.

"Okay then. So, what happened after you came to from your fainting spell?"

I close my eyes, taking a deep breath to steady myself, and try to picture everything that's happened over the past two hours.

Shit! Has it only been two hours? Where's Sarah? What's going on? Who has her?

My hands are trembling as I explain what happened in the mall's security room.

"Now, I've no idea what's going on. We need to wait for Kevin to come back after sucking up and playing all the cultural niceties. How's that for bullshit? Our daughter's been taken, and they're … they're sitting around, shaking hands, saying, *salaam alaikum* …"

I gulp down the rest of the amber fluid and stand. It takes effort, as my head throbs. I lied when Jacquie asked if I was okay. I'm not. My equilibrium is off, and it hurts to even think.

"Anika's right, too, you know," I murmur.

"What do you mean?"

"Women and kids are snatched all the time from this region. Sure, not Dubai per se, but from the Middle East, North Africa, and South Asia. I've seen some of the United Nations reports. They take pretty young girls and force them into prostitution rings. Sarah could be on her way to a Russian brothel now. Fuck!"

I stumble toward the pool and lean against the door. The glass is cool on my head. The blue from the pool lights gives off an eerie glow to the backyard. Usually watching the bugs fly around the bougainvillea-lined concrete walls enclosing the small area provides a semblance of calm. It's not working now.

I turn as Jacquie calls for my attention.

"Sarah's been missing only a few hours. You can't let your maid's fears affect your mindset. I doubt very much she's in a Russian brothel. Even if human traffickers have her, the authorities won't let them leave the Emirates."

"You don't know that. You don't. There are brothels right here, in this city. You know that, right?"

"There are rumors, but prostitution is against the law, so that's all they are."

"Oh, wise up, Jacquie," I snap. "They aren't rumors. There's a fucking brothel in al-Satwa, and I know because Kevin ended up there one night after wining and dining some Lebanese clients. He had no idea what was in the building and thought it was an exclusive bar until they started parading the girls out like conveyer-belt sushi."

"What?"

I don't know if her exclamation is for the prostitutes or their patrons. She should know about this. A lot of her shadier clientele frequent these places, I expect.

"I know, right? So, don't give me all this *against the law* bullshit. It all happens here. You just need to know who to pay or what to say. It's all a fine line and up to your interpretation of the Koran as to whether or not it is illegal. For Christ's sake, that Arab family the other month pretty much sold their daughter off to one of the sheikh's advisers, and how old was she? Twelve?" I bury my face in my hands. "Twelve years old. Poor girl. Gets her first period, and she's called a woman and shuffled off to be married to some horny old bastard."

"Jen, that's not what's happening to Sarah—"

"No, Jacquie. You don't know that. You don't. I'm not sure if you actually see the dirty underbelly of this place. Sarah's a pretty Caucasian girl with blonde hair and blue eyes. Ripe for the picking for some dirty, disgusting pedophile. You know what? She's probably not on her way to a Russian brothel. She's probably being picked up by those disgusting Asians. Maybe a Golden Triangle pedophile ring or … it would've been easy for them to have some Filipino woman on the payroll. Oh my God, maybe …"

I collapse down into the couch, head throbbing, heart dying. I'm haunted by the image captured by the mall's surveillance camera of Sarah being taken by that woman. I vaguely hear Jacquie leave the room before returning to place something on the coffee table in front of me.

"Here, take these. They should help with the head. I can tell it's still hurting."

Two white pills and a glass of water sit in front of me. The alcohol helps numb the pain, but it's not enough. It's only working on the physical pain. I want something to help me deal with the pain caused by the images I have of Sarah when I think of where she could be right now.

I raise my hands to my head and gently remove the bandage. There's a small lump where I hit my head, but it's not bleeding. At least, there's no stickiness on my fingers. I throw the soiled bandage on the table and pick up the pills. At this point, anything will do to take a break from the pain. I opt to wash the pills down with the rest of the whisky instead of water. Finishing the glass, I place the tumbler back on the table with a clunk. No coaster. I snicker to myself, thinking of my more pretentious friends and their abhorrence to marks on their furniture. Such a stupid thought.

I raise my head to see Jacquie messing around with her phone.

"Any news yet?" I ask wearily, the words thick on my tongue. I should be checking my cell for messages, but my arms are too heavy.

"Nothing good by the looks of it." Seeing my stricken face, she amends, "Nothing bad either. Alerts have gone out. The police are monitoring everything. Kevin's on his way home, and he should be here soon."

"Thanks, Jacquie," I slur. "What would I do without you?"

"Thankfully, you'll never have to find that out."

A door slamming at the front of the villa has her up and moving. Judging by the ear-piercing level of chatter, Kevin has arrived and is talking to someone either in his office or on the phone. Then, there's silence, save for the hum from the pool's filtration system.

Heels clicking on the tiled hallway signal Jacquie's return. I look up and see the concern etched on her face.

"Kevin's home. No more news."

"Oh" is all I can manage as I struggle to keep my eyes open.

We sit and wait in silence, watching the water ripple on the pool.

"Shit, Jacquie, what did you give her?" Kevin asks as he enters the room and stands in front of me.

"Just some painkillers for her headache and some Xanax to calm her down."

"And some whisky," Kevin adds, sniffing one of the empty glasses.

"I thought it best. She wasn't doing too well. I fed Liam and sent him to bed a few hours ago." Jacquie stands in front of Kevin and places a sympathetic hand on his arm. "Oh my God, Kevin. What's really going on? From what Jen said and saw, it sounds planned, like a conspiracy."

With the whisky bottle and another glass in hand, Kevin throws a concerned glance my way before sitting down. My eyes are heavy. The drugs Jacquie gave me, mixed with the alcohol, have succeeded in making me numb. I can barely keep my eyes open. Each blink lasts a second longer until my eyelids are glued shut. The noises around me start to fade, but I listen to their discussion, cursing my weakness of not being present enough to be of any help.

"I'm not too sure. The Dubai Police, our embassy, and Interpol are on it. The embassy's released some details to the media, which sure as hell won't go over well. The local authorities are going to be livid."

"But what was all that stuff about a monitoring station at the mall?" Jacquie asks.

"Yeah, that's screwed up. Apparently, the Emiratis have invested heavily in electronic surveillance in all public places. Big brother is watching you and all that. Though, today, I'm thankful. They were able to track Sarah through the video feeds. We've a few stills of at least three of the people involved. I gave these to the embassy, who are passing them to Interpol."

"Okay, that's good news. Something positive at least."

"Yes. It should help track them down. Now, we just sit and wait. The authorities are ruling out a kidnapping for ransom, but we don't know for sure. They've released a number for people to call. If it's for ransom, we should hear something within the next day or so. Until then, we have no choice but to trust them to find our daughter."

7

———

"Jen! Jen!"

I draw in a breath, and it's like I'm sucking in jagged glass. I must have been sleeping with my mouth open, as it's dry and stiff. My eyes open slowly, contradicting the urgency of the summons, the effort painful.

"Jen?" A hand gently shakes my shoulder but finishes as a caress down my arm.

Eyes finally open, I find myself staring into Kevin's solemn gray ones. A sad smile flits over his face as he cups my cheek with his hand.

"The embassy staff is here. They're setting up in my office, and they need to talk to both of us. You up to it, or are those drugs that Jacquie gave you still working?"

Embassy staff? Sarah!

I sit up as the hideous memories flood back. My head throbs, but it's not as bad as earlier.

"Sarah?" I ask anxiously, not masking my fear.

"Nothing yet. I'm hoping, once they set up their equipment, they'll give us an update on what's happening." He runs a hand over his unshaven chin, his eyes reflecting the worry of mine.

"How long has it been? How long was I out?"

"Only an hour or so."

I reach up and place my hand over his, connecting us. "Okay. Someone's here, you said?"

"Yes, specialists from the embassy. They're going to help us with the ransom demand once they come through."

"Ransom? So, they think it was a kidnapping?" The fear I was holding back gradually begins to bubble to the surface.

"Yes, they do. It'll be better if they explain everything. Come on. We both need to talk to them."

"I need to brush my teeth. I feel like I have cotton mouth."

"You've time. Go grab a shower. You still have dried blood on you from the mall. Anika's brewing some coffee. It'll be ready by the time you're back down."

I nod and try to push myself to my feet. Kevin stands from his crouched position in front of me and offers his hand. It's an effort, but I make it to standing. My head throbs, but it's a little better. Kevin lets go once I am steady and prepares to leave the room.

"Is Jacquie still here?"

He stills and looks over his shoulder. "No. She left not long after you passed out. She promised to check in with me later."

"She didn't want to stay?" I look away from Kevin to mask my response as my voice trails off with uncertainty.

"She did. She just thought she could help by researching kidnapping cases in the area and reviewing the local laws pertaining to it. In case we have legal questions. I called Melanie, and she's on her way over."

"Okay, that's good."

"Don't be long, okay? They'll have everything set up soon."

―――――

I'm hardly through the threshold of Kevin's office before a tall man in a lightweight gray suit is shaking my hand and ushering me to the IKEA two-seater under the side window.

"Mrs. Johnson, please take a seat. My name is George Bailey. I'm the regional security officer with the US Embassy."

George runs his hands through his dark hair and tugs at the collar of what looks to be an expensive dress shirt.

"Jennifer. Please call me Jennifer, and I don't want to sit. I want to know what's happening. Is there any news?" I'm exhausted, and my head hurts. I just want answers. *Where is Sarah, and what do the people who have her want with her? And when can we get her back?*

"Not as of yet. Please take a seat, and I'll run through what we have so far."

I reluctantly sink into the chair as Kevin enters the room with two steaming cups of coffee. He hands me a cup and sits next to me. The equipment George and his subordinate have set up has turned Kevin's office into something akin to a police investigation center. I didn't notice the large mobile whiteboard propped up in front of the bookshelf when I walked in. The still shots taken from the MOE's security room have been taped at the top. Below them are other photos showing vehicles and a blurred photo of a man. George and his team have used red and black markers to link photos together and write in what appears to be the times and locations.

"Who is that? Does he have Sarah?" I ask, studying the photo.

"At the moment, we're unsure. As you can see, the Emirati surveillance has been able to track Sarah's abductors from the mall to a small warehouse in al-Quoz. It looks like the Filipino who took her from the store was just the hook to take her from the mall. Once she got Sarah into the waiting vehicle, she left and has disappeared.

"The vehicle's windows were tinted, and we couldn't identify the people inside from the images shared by the Dubai Police, but we think your daughter was in the vehicle. We were lucky to get that image. It's just a pity the profile of the driver is distorted. He appears to be of Arab origin, but it's hard to tell from that angle.

"Based on the way Sarah was abducted, we believe she was kidnapped and will be held for ransom. Your husband has been negotiating an important deal in Iraq with the Kurds, and plenty of groups aren't too happy about it."

"You think Sarah was kidnapped because of Kevin's work?"

What? Did he know that this was a possibility? That this would happen? What kind of business deals is he negotiating?

"Possibly—"

I cut George off as I stand. I'm confused. Some of the words from his briefing play back in my mind.

Al-Quoz is a mixed industrial and residential area on the eastern side of Sheikh Zayed Road. It's not far from the Mall of the Emirates or even our Jumeirah villa.

"Hang on, you said they're in a warehouse in al-Quoz? You know where she is? Why haven't we gotten her back yet?" I quickly spit the words out, hoping the answer will come back just as fast.

George looks at Kevin, who's standing next to me, hand on my shoulder. I see a flash of pity in George's eyes before I turn my attention to my husband.

"Jen, George hasn't finished. Sit down and let him finish so we can start discussing our options."

"Yes, sorry," George starts. He runs his hands through his close-cropped dark hair again, closes his eyes, and takes a deep breath. He's frustrated; I can see that now. "I should have explained that a bit better. So far, we've been relying on Emirati intelligence and information regarding this, and they've been cooperative up to a point.

"Yes, Sarah was tracked to the warehouse in al-Quoz, but by the time we were informed, she'd already been moved. The Dubai Police did go in, but we think they already knew she wasn't there before they conducted the raid. As to where she's been moved to, we—the embassy—have no idea. The locals haven't told us whether they've picked anything up from their surveillance systems."

"But, obviously, if they could track a vehicle there, they'd know if one left?" Kevin asks intently, placing his coffee mug on the side table.

"Exactly, but we don't know. They haven't shared the information. Everything we know to date is from their initial briefing."

"Why?" I allow anger and frustration to bleed into my voice. "Why the hell aren't they sharing the information? What are they doing? Are they actually taking it seriously?"

"Yes, Mrs. Johnson. They are. The entire Dubai Police Force and other local agencies are on high alert. This is currently their number one priority. They want it resolved as swiftly as you do … as we all do." George leans against Kevin's desk, rubbing his forehead. "I have an officer at their police headquarters keeping an eye on things and reporting back to me. Trouble is, although we have a pretty good relationship with the Dubai authorities and the Emirati government, it doesn't mean they'll work with us on this. We do know they take their security and their laws seriously, so we just need to wait and see. My staffer, who is there as a liaison, has a good working relationship with the police and security government officials."

Just wait and see? I forcibly set my empty coffee mug down on the table. *Just wait and see?*

"You want us to just wait and see? You realize that's what you're asking us to do?" I snap, raising my hand to silence George's response. "Wait … and see. Our daughter's gone. You need to be doing more than waiting."

"I'm sorry, Mrs. Johnson. Of course we are. We'll be putting as much pressure on the Emiratis that we can to get answers."

I scrunch my eyebrows in annoyance, thinking about the local police and officials, and turn to Kevin. "Why did he say earlier that this could be a kidnapping due to your work?"

Briefly, Kevin gazes at the colorful Iranian carpet at our feet, clearly upset at my accusatory tone. His hands, which were previously resting on his thighs, are now clenched tight into fists with whitened knuckles. With pursed lips, he shakes his head before taking a deep breath.

"I've been negotiating with the Kurdish government for oil and gas exploration opportunities. We're representing an international oil company headquartered in the US, and the Iraqi government as well as several extremist groups are unhappy with us. The political stakes are high, and we've received a few threats. Basically, the Iraqis don't want us doing deals with the Kurds, as it's seen as undermining Baghdad's authority over the country."

I sit up straighter in my seat. It's the first I've heard about this. I don't really pay much attention to Kevin's work other than when he's traveling or at some conference that gets in the way of my day-to-day life. I note the absences, but we rarely discuss his work. He keeps most of it to himself, and to be honest, I'm not sure we'd have the time to talk about it in detail, as we spend our "together" time as a family. Our time is extremely limited due to his long hours and business trips. I know he deals with most of the Arab governments and their energy ministries, as I pay attention just enough when we're out at work-related functions. But the Kurds ... and threats?

"Threats? Like what? What does it mean?" I ask, my voice hitching on the end of my question.

"It means ..." He glances quickly at George before turning to me. "It means we've received threats. They've threatened our safety if we keep up with our Kurdish negotiations."

"Whose safety? The safety of your business dealings? Your staff in the field or in your office? Or the safety of your family?" I demand.

I stand and start pacing the length of the office while George and Kevin watch me. I stop in front of the desk and bang my fists before turning to glare at Kevin. I'm furious. I can't believe he knew there were threats against our family, however indirectly, and he didn't see fit to share them. I can't believe I'm just now hearing about this after our daughter has been kidnapped. Possibly by Iraqi extremists and government agents, no less.

"Why am I hearing about this only now? How long have you known this could happen? We could have stayed in the US if we'd known."

"Calm down, Jen. Threats like this are a dime a dozen and come hand in hand with working in the region. These risks are part of the deal." Kevin sits back in the chair, watching me pace.

"No. I'm not going to be calm. Threats to us, to our family, should be taken seriously."

He shakes his head, clearly frustrated with me. "And they are. That's what the security section does. They look into them and do their thing. You know we can't travel into an area or do anything without their knowledge or clearance. You know this. As my wife, you were given training by our team."

"Then, how did they let it get to the point that Sarah was taken? How? Are you blaming me? Is that it?"

George moves in front of the whiteboard. "There's no confirmation that the people who took Sarah are related to Kevin's work. We're trying to cover all the bases here. It's a possibility, and it's all we've got to go on at the moment. What we do know is, the abductors were well organized and knew enough of the Dubai Police surveillance network to avoid identification. They also knew enough about law enforcement response times and methods to slip detection. This suggests Sarah was taken for a specific purpose and it wasn't some random abduction. Until we get a demand, we won't know the who or the why."

He shoots a glance at his assistant, who has spent this entire time behind computer equipment at Kevin's desk. The assistant acknowledges him and slightly shakes his head.

George sighs and faces us again. "We don't have any new information yet, which isn't necessarily a bad thing. It just means the Emiratis are continuing with their investigations and we haven't been updated yet." He grabs the back of his neck with his right hand and briefly closes his eyes.

"Our hands are tied with that side of things. Basing our assumption that Sarah was kidnapped for a reason, we need to wait this out until either the Emiratis find her or we receive a ransom demand. And that's why Don is here," George says, indicating his assistant. "He set up the equipment to monitor your landline and cell phones. When we receive the ransom demand, we'll be able to record it as well as possibly track the caller's location, depending on the method they use to contact us. Same if they initiate contact through email or a social media site. Don will be able to derive information from the metadata, and we can use it along with other intelligence to track Sarah."

Don looks up from his computer and provides a tight smile at his introduction. As George continues his briefing, Don continues with his work.

"Several FBI agents experienced in crisis negotiation, specifically kidnappings, are on their way as we speak. Kevin, your office is sending their crisis-response consultant to deal with any ransom demands. Assuming this *is* a straight kidnapping operation targeting an expat, we don't really need him here with myself, Don, and the FBI engaged. However, it's a requirement under your and your company's insurance guidelines. If all of this is assessed as having a commercial or political motivation, he'll be here to negotiate that on behalf of your company. He'll also act as the liaison between us and their legal team."

George takes a deep breath and moves in front of the whiteboard, studying the images.

"Finally," he continues, "as you are probably aware, if this situation somehow escalates and demands are made of the US government, it could become categorized as a terrorist-related event, and … well, let's just hope it doesn't escalate, as it'll tie the hands of the insurers in regard to paying any ransom."

"How will they know to contact us?" I ask, voice strained. My question sounds rather loud and distorted to my ears. The coffee I finished has left a bitter taste in my mouth.

All this talk about political interests, negotiators, FBI, and insurance payouts is too much. I just want Sarah back.

Exhaustion hits me as I get a bout of vertigo and stumble slightly. I manage to flop into my chair before I fall. The day's events, combined with the pills and the too-short nap, are taking their toll. Whatever adrenaline I've been running on since Kevin woke me is wearing off fast.

"What time is it anyway?" I speak my thought aloud.

"It's almost 11:00 p.m.," Kevin answers me, rubbing my shoulder in support.

"We believe they'll contact you directly. All indicators point to it being a professional kidnapping, so they know who you are. They know who to contact to gain either the leverage they want or the cash payout. Worst case, Sarah can give them your details." George answers my former question as he studies the timeline on the whiteboard, his fingers tapping on the first still of Sarah walking out of the mall with the Filipino maid. "It's been approximately five hours and forty minutes since she was taken. We've got seventy-two hours for them to contact us."

"Seventy-two hours? Why seventy-two hours?" Kevin asks the question before I can.

George turns, his face pale in contrast with his tan hand that rubs his jaw. He clears his throat before answering. "If the kidnappers don't reach out within the seventy-two-hour window, it's possible we've miscalculated the intent of the kidnapping, and the chance of getting Sarah back is highly diminished."

The world falls out from beneath me for the second time today. This is madness.

A cell phone echoes in the quiet room. George looks at us with an apology in his eyes as he moves to the far corner of the office to answer the call in a hushed voice. Kevin wraps his arms around me as his lips brush over my temple.

"What are we going to do, Kevin? What are we going to do?"

"I don't think there's anything we can do, except wait. We'll have everything in place and be ready when they call."

"If they call …" I shudder at the alternative.

"They'll call, Jen. They have to."

8

───────

I'm sitting in the back room by the pool, waiting—but probably more correctly, hiding.

After George explained what would likely happen and what we needed to do to prepare for the ransom demand, our villa turned into Kidnap Headquarters Central. His staff has effectively taken over the front half of the villa, encompassing Kevin's office and the guest bedroom and bathroom. The doorbell was working overtime for a while with all the comings and goings. At first, I was worried with all the activity and associated noise that it would wake Liam. As I've always known, the boy can sleep through anything. Or maybe his slumber could be attributed to Jacquie giving him Dramamine to calm him down and help him sleep when I was passed out earlier. I can't believe she did that.

Who hands out drugs like party favors—and to kids?

I shake my head as if that will clear the haze and try to put my thoughts in some form of order. Jacquie gave us drugs yesterday, not today. Although we're still in the first twenty-four hours of Sarah's abduction, we've now moved into the second day.

I close my eyes and bring Rosie—Sarah's toy snow leopard—up to my cheek, rubbing its plush fur against my face. Rosie smells of Sarah, and a warmth spreads through me as I acknowledge this. Rosie was her third birthday gift from Kevin and me. Sarah's love for cats made Rosie an immediate favorite, and they haven't spent a night apart since. After our initial briefing with the embassy staff, I found Rosie, determined the soft toy would not spend the night alone. It might sound ridiculous, but I know Sarah would want that.

The FBI team in charge of negotiations arrived an hour ago, having flown in from Kuwait, and the crisis-response consultant from Kevin's office arrived shortly after. Anika moved a small camping table from our storeroom into the office along with most of our dining chairs. I don't understand why they didn't just set up in the dining room or use both of the spaces. I mentioned this to Kevin, and he said it had something to do with the security of information and privacy. The office has double doors that can be closed and locked along with blackout curtains. It's also the only soundproof room in the house.

When we moved into the villa with its high ceilings and tiled floors, we knew noise would carry. We soundproofed the office and media room as much as possible by placing carpets on the floor and hanging some on the walls. We didn't want Kevin to be distracted by household noise when working in the office. The Persian carpets we'd purchased from the Blue Souk were stunning. Kevin had been ecstatic at the prices he negotiated, just a fraction of the US retail cost. I always enjoyed our family outings to the Blue Souk in Sharjah. The kids especially loved the trinkets while I loved watching Kevin try to smooth-talk and barter with the vendors.

The door opening startles me, forcing me from my reverie, and Rosie falls to my lap. It takes but a glance to identify the intruder before I'm up and in her arms.

"Melanie. I'm so glad you're here. God, I need you right now."

She wraps me in a warm embrace and holds tightly as I quietly sob into her shoulder. Our friendship has spanned the five years we've spent living in Dubai. A seasoned expat, Melanie helped me navigate the choppy cultural waters during those initial frustrating months after our move. It was my luckiest day when she chose to stand under the shade of a tree on the school campus and start up a conversation with me while I waited for the school day to end.

"Shush. I'm so sorry I couldn't get here sooner. Frank was in London, and his flight returned only an hour ago. Yolanda's not back until tomorrow, and I didn't have anyone to keep an eye on Jonathan. I hope you're not mad at me." Her sweet Southern drawl hints at her worry.

"Not at all. It's been pretty hectic with all the various security people coming in to advise and prepare us for a ransom demand."

Melanie takes my hands and moves me back to the lounge; she doesn't let go as we sit. "Kevin updated me on the situation, and I'm here for you, darling. So, ransom demand?" She phrases it as a question, but I can see the wheels of her mind turning as she assesses me.

"Yes." I briefly turn my head away from her. The kindness and caring I see in her eyes makes my chest tighten. I unclasp one of my hands from hers and tug at my ear, trying to swallow back the nausea leaping to my throat. My voice comes out shaky. "It's my fault. I shouldn't have been at the mall. I shouldn't have been in Carrefour with the kids at that time of the day."

"Jen, look at me. I know you're feeling all sorts of guilt right now, but it's not your fault. Kevin took me in the office when I got here. I've seen the boards that the embassy staff is working on. They said it looks like a professional kidnapping. That means you were targeted. If it wasn't Carrefour yesterday, it might have been Magic Planet today."

She squeezes my hand in assurance before she continues in a softer voice. "Sarah needs your strength now. There's no time for guilt or blame. She needs you focused. As do Liam and Kevin. You're the strength and backbone of this family. If you crumble, they won't know what to do. Christ, men are pathetic at the best of times."

I choke on a laugh as my tears continue to fall silently, her dig at men in general getting the response she intended. This is why I love Melanie and why she should've been here in the beginning instead of Jacquie. She's uniquely sweet and generous, and she hasn't been tainted by her time spent living within the expat bubble. Her calming influence is what I need, and she's right; I do have to be strong for all of them.

I use the back of my sleeve to wipe away the last of my tears.

Melanie notices my hands shaking with the action and frowns. She takes them in hers again. "When was the last time you had something to eat?"

"Um …" I squint my eyes at her as I try to remember. "Yesterday morning maybe? Morning tea with Monica and Kate at Lime Tree?"

"You're joking with me right now, aren't you?"

I shake my head, and despite myself, a small smile forces its way to my lips. If there's one thing Melanie can't abide, it's people not eating properly. She stands, flicking the imaginary lint from her pants as she does. Wrinkling her brow, she looks at me.

"Well then, I best be fixing that. Kevin's associate Jacquie brought you home, right?"

"Yes. She gave me some whisky and Xanax and let me pass out on the couch here. I've had about three coffees since Kevin woke me," I say, watching her for her reaction.

I'm not disappointed as she shakes her head, mumbling not-so-nice things about Jacquie. There's no love lost between them, and it's just as well that Jacquie only socializes with us at work-related functions.

"Well then, you head upstairs and clean yourself up. I'll make breakfast, and we can work out a plan for the next few days. I told Frank I'd be here as long as you needed me." She leaves the room, heading toward the kitchen. "The sun will be up in a few hours. You need to decide if Liam's going to school. I'll see you in a few. Don't take too long."

I rest my head on the back of the couch and stare at the ceiling. Melanie wants to plan out the next few days, but I'm not too sure for what. We're effectively sitting around, either waiting on the Emiratis to provide us with an update on their investigation or for the ransom demand.

The call to prayer from the mosque on the street behind us booms over the loudspeaker, its sound cathartic for the turmoil raging in my mind. Melanie's right; the sun will be up in a few hours to welcome the new day, forcing Ramadan's restrictions back on us.

I sit up, looking for Rosie in between the cushions. My hand involuntarily starts petting the toy, and the connection I felt earlier with Sarah comes back. I bend over to inhale her scent as the queasiness in my stomach returns.

With a final sniff, I stand, resolute. I'm no good to Sarah like this. I have to get my act together. I need to be strong for my family, friends, and Sarah. For that to happen, I need to stop hiding in the back room, wallowing in self-pity. I need to start taking action. No way am I going to let the US Embassy, FBI, or the crisis-response consultant make any decisions without me. Melanie said I needed to stop with the guilt. What's done is done. I need to move on.

The decisions and choices I make now and moving forward will define who I want to be as a person and as a mother. This isn't about me. It's about Sarah. I can't let her down. I will fight for her to bring her home, safe and sound.

With my mind made up, I hurry upstairs to take a shower, my second in four hours.

This time, when I head back downstairs, I'm prepared for the day. I'm prepared to do everything it will take to get my Sarah back. Damn the consequences.

9

———

"Any updates?" I ask the crisis-response team as I enter the office with a takeaway tray filled with Costa Coffee and a brown paper bag.

Yesterday, we had a meeting, discussing how we should be seen from outside the villa. The consensus and recommendation from the group of security specialists was to appear as normal as possible, which meant work for Kevin and school for Liam. It also meant these two additional areas were a possible avenue for the kidnappers to get a message to us. If we continued to close ranks and fortify ourselves in the villa, surrounded by security, we'd run the risk of scaring the kidnappers off or missing any signals they might try to send.

It's hard to pretend like everything's normal. The knots in my stomach have increased with every passing hour that we've heard nothing. That we have done nothing.

I remained in the villa for most of the day, leaving only for a short time to take Liam to school. We informed the school of Sarah's abduction, and they promised to keep the information confidential for the moment. The school increased the campus alert status to amber on the recommendation from the US Embassy with a statement of an identified increased threat to US expats. The embassy's security staff wasn't too worried about the safety of the school, as the new ASD campus in al-Barsha had been purposely built to meet high security standards. It was as secure as Fort Knox on a normal day, let alone when operating at an elevated threat level.

Fat lot of good it did Sarah.

Melanie collected Liam from school. She was also thoughtful enough to bring the refreshments for everyone currently camped out in our villa. The aroma emanating from the brown paper bag was mouthwatering and hinted to Costa's signature toasted sandwiches.

"Nope. You?" Craig, the FBI crisis negotiator, responds, looking up from behind his computer screen. His eyes light up, and a smile breaks out on his face when he sees the goodies I'm carrying. "Outstanding. I'm starving. I swear, your crisis headquarters is much better than the last one we were housed at in Kuwait."

I stop and look at him, mouth agape and eyes wide.

Craig's whole demeanor changes. He hunches his shoulders and appears to shrink into himself. He looks down at his feet as they scuff the floor before slowly raising his head to meet my gaze. "Sorry, Jen. I didn't mean that to come out the way it did. You'd think, in my line of work, I'd be more adept at not putting my foot in my mouth. I'm sorry for appearing insensitive."

I briefly close my eyes and plaster on a fake smile. *Strong. I need to be strong.*

I've learned some interesting things in the last forty-eight hours. I knew kidnapping was a big economic earner in some countries, but I wasn't aware of how popular it was and how the trend had taken off in Iraq with Western citizens as well as local businessmen being targeted for ransom payouts. Taylor, Craig's deputy from the FBI, told me earlier that some people were taken for ideological reasons, but they were the minority despite what mainstream media would have us believe. She said the monetary-driven kidnappings were more than likely carried out by similar groups with money paid going toward weapons and equipment to further their cause and expand regional networks. Everything I've seen or heard in the past forty-eight hours belongs in a Hollywood thriller, not in the front room of my home.

"No, that's okay, Craig. Here, take a coffee before it gets cold. And a sandwich as well."

"Thanks." His embarrassed and somewhat ashamed expression acts as an apology for his insensitive comment.

Craig returns to his seat with his coffee and sandwich. I turn my attention to George, who was napping on the two-seater couch. He yawns, and some of his joints crack as he stretches before attempting to straighten his rumpled clothes.

"I hope some of that's for me," he says, eyeing the coffee.

"Of course. Melanie dropped it off with Liam. There's more. Where's the rest of the team?"

Craig sticks his head back up from his work. "Don's asleep in your guest bedroom, and I think Taylor headed up to the back room by the pool to watch some television. She said Don was snoring and she couldn't sleep in there with him."

After the initial first twelve hours when everyone got situated and set up their equipment, they've been working in shifts, apart from the corporate crisis-response consultant supporting the interests of Kevin's insurance company. After receiving briefings at the Dubai Police operational center and from the embassy staff here in our villa, he headed back to his hotel after leaving his contact details with George.

I am extremely grateful for Taylor's presence. She took the time to go through all the information and analysis with me and explained all the possible scenarios as well as gave me an idea of the actions they would probably take for each. That did wonders for my anxiety. Some of the scenarios weren't very nice to listen to, but having the information was better than not.

Having Taylor here and seeing her fortitude in dealing with the situation, knowing she's dealt with much worse, has helped me put everything into perspective. I also like her because she's a straight shooter. I feel she'll always tell me how it is, and she won't attempt to soften the blow. She doesn't see me as someone needing to hide from the truth, and as I see the strength in her, I know she sees the same in me. I'll fight now and deal with the emotional backlash when it's over and I have Sarah back in my arms where she belongs.

There's a content glow on George's face as he takes a long sip of coffee and sighs. He takes up residence at Kevin's desk and scrolls through his computer. "The security team at ASD reports nothing out of the ordinary occurred at the school today. No suspicious vehicles, and only two people checked in at the security gate, requesting a visitor's pass because they'd left theirs at home. Both were in the school's database," he says, his eyes never leaving the screen. His fingers click on the keyboard as he puts down the coffee and sits up straight.

A cell phone rings, and George picks his up and answers immediately. "Yes. Yes. I've just seen it. Yes, I understand. We'll see you soon."

Clearing his throat, he says, "That was Eric, my liaison with the Dubai Police." After a minute of intense concentration, he studies me for a moment before continuing, "The Dubai Police have picked up the Filipino who took Sarah from the mall. This is good. Craig, Eric sent through the initial report. Have you received it?"

"Reading it now."

George's eyes remain on mine as I place down the food and coffee on an empty bookshelf beside the whiteboard. My heart is pounding, and I wring my hands, feeling the clamminess of my palms. This information sounds encouraging. I want to be excited about it, but something in George's demeanor is putting me on edge.

I want to ask him what it means, but the words momentarily stick in my throat. It takes effort to force them out, and when I manage to make the words, they're stuttered. "Wh-wh-what does this mean? This is good news, isn't it?" I'm sure the confusion is written all over my face.

He nods slowly. It's been two days since Sarah was taken, and there hasn't been any attempted contact by the kidnappers. From my understanding, the embassy has been meeting with the Dubai Police on our behalf for the latest updates, which, up until now, was nothing except dead ends.

"Yes, it could be good news," George replies slowly, looking away from me as Craig gets up and exits the room.

He's not telling me something. I can sense it.

"We'll contact the Emiratis and ask for the interview transcripts. Hopefully, they will find out who hired her or whom she was working with. If we get really lucky, she might know where they are."

The problem, as I have learned from Taylor, is the Dubai Police are *not* very good with sharing information. She told me George and his team have had issues with getting more than just cursory updates. Sure, Lieutenant Ahmed has let them in on the meetings, but nothing of substance has been discussed.

My hands tremble, and I take a seat when the other team members return to the room. Taylor gives my shoulder a quick squeeze as she walks past to the desk space Craig vacated. Don arrives, rubbing his eyes, trying to stifle a yawn. He perks up as he sees the abandoned coffee and gives me a nod as he takes a cup and goes to check his computer and equipment.

"Do you think her arrest will hinder or hasten the kidnappers contacting us?" I ask carefully.

The silence in the room unnerves me. They don't seem too excited about this development, not as excited as I was initially.

There's a moment of hesitation before anyone attempts to answer or even look in my direction.

George clears his throat as he picks up some paperwork on the desk, only to put it back down. "We're not sure, Jennifer. It really depends on—" He pauses, and my heart jumps a beat. "—the circumstances of her arrest and, obviously, the information she has."

"Okay, and …" I trail off, hoping one of them will give me something more.

Craig takes a seat in one of the dining room chairs alongside me. "What George is trying to say is, don't get your hopes up. We'll obviously know more when Eric arrives, but from reading his report and interpretation of the arrest, it might not be the good news you're hoping for."

"And?" I prompt, fidgeting in my seat.

Why don't they just spit it out and tell me?

"And," Taylor continues, "depending on the circumstances of the arrest, they might have screwed up any plans the kidnappers already made. Normally, this could be good, but since the abductors haven't reached out and identified themselves or made their demands … well, they could decide the risk is too high now and abandon their plans."

"Taylor!" George reprimands.

"What? She has a right to know," Taylor challenges. With a softer voice, she turns to me and continues. "That's if the kidnapping was for purely monetary reasons. The majority of the time, this type of kidnapper won't put themselves at risk. If they're a professional syndicate, they might decide the risk versus the reward is not worth it and forsake it. They'll probably weigh up the risks of being identified alongside their moral constitution and make a decision as to how to … deal with the hostage."

At my sharp intake of breath, Craig glares at Taylor. "Listen, Jen, Taylor's right—or what I mean is, she could be right. We won't know until Eric briefs us and answers our questions. Take a deep breath. There's no bad news here. It's all good. It means we'll have answers soon—hopefully, followed by a resolution."

I nod, and my stomach knots. "Okay. How long until Eric gets here?"

"He'll be here before *iftar*," George answers.

It gives us a twenty-minute wait.

I nod to myself and stand, ready to leave the room. "Okay. Good. I'll let Kevin know. He should be on his way home from work anyway," I say to no one in particular as I cross over the threshold, prepared to face whatever comes next.

10

———

I greet Kevin at the front door. Eric hasn't arrived yet, and I take the opportunity to drag him upstairs and fill him in on the situation as I understand it. I quietly close the bedroom door behind us.

"Why can't we do this downstairs, Jen? At least then I can have a drink. God, I need a drink," Kevin says, clearly annoyed.

Kevin drops his briefcase on the bed and walks over to stare out the back window overlooking the balcony off our room. His hands are clenched behind his head. I follow his gaze and see the Burj Khalifa. It's so tall that even at a distance of three miles, as the crow flies, it looks as though it could be a block away.

"Because I need to talk to you about what's going on, and George and his team have pretty much taken over the entire downstairs. It's more private up here," I reply slowly, not understanding why I should be pleading with him for his time.

Things between us were strange after the kids and my return from summer break. With everything currently going on, I can't work out if his behavior should be attributed to his work or Sarah.

"And why do you need to tell me what's going on? Isn't that their job?" He lets his arms fall to his sides and turns to face me, eyes devoid of emotion.

I furrow my brows and blink in confusion. *Where's this aggression coming from?* Frustration and impatience, I can understand, but annoyance and anger, I'm not too sure.

"What's the matter, Kevin?" I ask gently, slowly walking to him and placing my hands on his chest.

He closes his eyes and sighs as he moves his forehead down to rest against mine. "Nothing's the matter." He chuckles, but it sounds strained. Forced. "Other than the obvious, nothing's the matter. I'm sorry. It's just been a hectic day at work, filled with meeting after meeting. And none of it matters; none of it compares to what's going on here."

I take his face in my hands and stare into his eyes as they tear up. "I'm sorry, too. I was going to ask you about your day and how it went, keeping up the pretense in the office."

It's painful to see him hurting like this. He takes me in his arms, and my hair sticks to the wetness on his face as he rubs it against me. While my tears soak the front of his shirt, a lump in my throat forms, and my voice cracks as I try to speak. "To be honest, I'm a bit jealous. It sounds like being at work was difficult, but at least it was a distraction. Every time one of them took a phone call, left the office, or even when they were talking among themselves, I was thinking, *This is it. Something has happened or is going to happen.* The waiting has been excruciating."

His lips slightly turn up before he places a quick kiss to my forehead. He releases me, wiping his eyes with his shirtsleeve before moving to the end of the bed and taking a seat. "Tell me. Tell me what's the latest from the home front."

I pull a few tissues from the box on my bedside table and scrub my face and nose. I take a seat next to him but scoot back until my shoulders hit the headboard and sit cross-legged, pulling Rosie out from under my pillow and sitting her in my lap. "Well, Liam had a good day at school. I think his distraction worked well for him. He's finished his homework and is playing the PS4 with his friends online. The school reported to the embassy that nothing unusual had happened, which was a relief. Melanie picked him up for me and brought him home."

Kevin grunts and inclines his head for me to go on.

"The security guys downstairs have been continuing working in shifts. Other than George, I don't think any of them have left the villa since they arrived. Eric, the liaison George has working with the Dubai Police, is on his way over. As I said on the phone, they arrested the woman who had taken Sarah from the mall. When Eric arrives, we'll find out more."

"Okay," Kevin says after he kicks his shoes off and scrunches backward to sit beside me.

"How was it in the office today?"

"I don't know. Strange. All the expats know what's going on but have been instructed to do and say nothing. Everyone's on high alert, and the families who don't have kids at ASD were told to stay home. Jacquie was in the building for a meeting, and we had lunch at the café downstairs. They've got it blacked out for Ramadan. It was a nightmare, completely packed, and every time someone walked past our table and knocked my chair, I thought it might be the kidnappers dropping off a message."

I take his hand and give it a squeeze. "I'm sure that felt overwhelming. I'm glad it wasn't me. I would've panicked."

"You probably would have," he says, smiling gently, no doubt trying to lessen the blow.

"How's Jacquie? I haven't heard from her since the other night. You know, when … she brought me home." I rest my head on the wall and close my eyes as I think back to how much of a mess I was that night. I'm still a mess, but at least I'm in control and functioning. "So much has happened in the past forty-eight hours, but at the same time, nothing's progressed. We still don't know where Sarah is, who has her, what they want with her, what they want from us, or even if she ... God forbid, whether she's dead or alive. I don't want to think like this, but I can't help it. It's been running through my mind as though on repeat."

"Jen—" Kevin says, turning toward me.

"No, no. I'm okay. I've just been trying to keep up a brave front for you, Liam, and Sarah. It's been great with the guys downstairs; they've been fantastic. I know we're in good hands with them, but I just can't help to think about how Sarah is feeling right now. Is she hot, or is she cold? Is she hungry? Have they been feeding her? I'm just worried about her well-being."

Kevin takes Rosie out of my hands and wraps his arms around me, and I taste the salt from my tears on my lips.

"Maybe this maid they arrested can answer our questions."

The doorbell chimes. We stiffen.

I leap from the bed. "Oh my God, that must be Eric."

"Great. Let's go get our answers," Kevin says, leaving the room to go downstairs.

I rub Rosie's head before I secret her away under my pillow once more. Then, I quickly step into the bathroom.

Puffy eyelids and bloodshot eyes from crying and lack of sleep stare back at me from my reflection. Cold water splashed on my face does nothing for my appearance but works to liven me up before I head downstairs to see what Eric has to say. I hope and pray it's good news.

II

It's been over forty-eight hours, and there's been nothing … until now. The clock is continuing to count down toward the magical seventy-second hour George told us about. My stomach tightens as I allow myself to think about what will happen if we reach seventy-two hours with no contact from the kidnappers. Kidnapping cases can be drawn out over weeks or months … sometimes, even as long as a year. I'm hoping and praying that the arrest of this Filipino woman will be the key to finding Sarah.

I hear the murmur of voices as I approach the office doors. Everyone is inside, and they're waiting for me. After taking a deep breath, I push the door open and see the concern on their faces. I hesitate before I step into the room. The pregnant pause as I enter makes me hold my breath, and I almost lose my composure.

Strong. I need to be strong.

"Jen, this is Eric. He's our liaison with the Dubai Police and Emirati government, and he has some information to brief us on," George says by way of introduction.

"Yes." I ignore Eric's hand held up in greeting. My throat is parched, and I struggle to swallow. "The Filipino maid—her arrest?"

I look to the other members of George's team, seeking some sort of indication as to what's going on. Something doesn't feel right. I'm missing something. Kevin is settled in the two-seater, a glass in his hand and a half-filled bottle of Glenlivet at his feet. He doesn't look at me, preferring to study the amber fluid in his glass. I stiffen at his disregard, wondering what happened between the intimate moment we shared five minutes ago and now. Craig and Don are studiously avoiding my gaze; apparently, their computer screens are a high priority at the moment. I look to Taylor, my straight shooter, and I see the pity in her eyes.

Fuck.

"Take a seat, Mrs. Johnson," Eric says, waving toward one of the chairs.

"My name is Jennifer, and I don't want to sit. I want to know what's going on," I reply through gritted teeth.

The irony of the déjà vu is not lost on me. Despite my words, I walk to Kevin and take his glass before taking a seat adjacent to him where I have full view of everyone in the room. He doesn't miss a beat, picking up the bottle and drinking straight from it.

George sighs, and rubbing the back of his neck, he gives Eric a nod to continue.

"I was on my way here from the police headquarters in al-Twar after receiving the briefing for the arrest of Dalisay Santos, the woman who had abducted your daughter, when I was called into a last-minute meeting." He turns to George, shaking his head in frustration. "I don't think it was their intention to invite me, but I happened to be talking to one of my contacts on the way out. Anyway, I have news, and it's not necessarily good."

Kevin brings the bottle back up to his lips and takes a deep drink. I blink, watching his throat work the liquid down. The smell wafting from the glass in my hand is making my stomach churn.

"Okay ..."

My word brings Eric's attention back to me.

Fumbling for his words, he takes a moment before he continues. "Apparently, the Emiratis have been busy. They raided a house in Sharjah yesterday, and the intel gathered led to Santos's arrest. I'm really sorry, but Sarah's abduction wasn't a kidnapping. There's not going to be a ransom call."

"What the fu—" I stand, the glass slipping from my hand, smashing as it hits the tiled floor and ricocheting in every direction. The sound echoes through the silent room as the distinct odor of whisky wafts behind it.

"It appears," George continues, "the Emiratis know more than they've been letting on. The house they raided in Sharjah had enough information to suggest they were collecting girls but not for ransom. They're a human-trafficking ring. And it appears Sarah's abduction was completely random. Santos's statement backs this up. She was paid for each girl she brought back. There was a sliding scale for payments, Caucasian girls being the top tier."

"You're saying Sarah was taken by this woman to meet a quota?" Kevin stares down Eric until he cringes.

"Yes, and—"

Kevin cuts Eric off and says in a robotic manner, "And this whole thing was wrong place, wrong time? If it wasn't Sarah, it would've been someone else?"

The spilled whisky on the floor pools around the shards of glass. I can see where Kevin's thoughts are going. Some of my tears dilute the liquid at my feet. I hiccup and wipe my face with the back of my hand.

Looking at the team assembled in the room, I ask the one question that hasn't been answered yet. "So, where's Sarah?"

"The reason I was actually allowed in the meeting was because the Dubai Police are in the process of closing the investigation. They've shut down this ring, as far as they're concerned. They also arrested a Russian man who was in the warehouse. He apparently has links to the Russian Mafia. They gave me copies of the interview reports for information and closure only."

"Where is Sarah?" I repeat my question, this time more fearful. My voice breaks.

"Jen," Taylor says, "they don't know. No one knows. They believe she's been taken out of the country on a black flight. The human-trafficking cell targets young woman and girls to sell into prostitution and slavery in Eastern Europe."

"No!"

I feel arms around me as I'm brought into the chest of a warm body. But it's not Kevin's arms or Kevin's chest being saturated with the result of my guilt and my fears. I'm in someone else's arms.

Kevin is sitting across the room as still as a statue, staring at me. He brings the bottle to his mouth and swallows the remaining amber liquid without breaking eye contact. He lets the bottle go, and it falls to the floor. His bottle doesn't smash like my glass. It lands, cushioned on the Persian carpet. It's anticlimactic. He breaks eye contact with me long enough to glance at the bottle before jumping up and kicking it into the wall. The last shard of glass hasn't settled before he turns and leaves the room.

My breath stutters as I inhale deeply. Everyone present is aware of my silent screams that suffocate me until no air is left in the room. With the front door slamming shut, I know Kevin has left the villa. Between my sobs, I only hope he'll come back. I've already lost so much. I won't survive losing anyone else.

12

It's been two days since the security team moved out. Watching them pack up their equipment and file their paperwork away was a bittersweet moment. Sweet for them, as they got to go back to their lives. Bitter for me because their departure confirmed my loss. It's as though the villa was professionally cleaned and all the life had been sucked out of it through the nozzle of a vacuum cleaner. And now that they've gone, I find myself existing in silence.

Anika goes about her chores in a detached manner, scurrying out of anyone's way and avoiding eye contact. Liam, when he's not at school, is locked in his room, absorbed in some form of electronics.

Kevin returned home the morning after his abrupt exit to change for work. I tried to talk to him, but he said he wasn't ready and was trying to consolidate the situation in his own mind before he could. It was heartbreaking because he wouldn't look at me. Although he was hungover and tired, I could tell anger bubbled away inside him, and I hoped it wasn't all directed at me. I'm trying to understand and give him space. I just wish we could talk through it together.

The FBI agents are rotating back to the US, and their replacements are not my concern. In fact, I have no reason to even meet them.

Before she left, Taylor took the time to talk to me in the straight manner that's purely her. She didn't hide the reality of my situation, giving me the statistics for missing persons in the area and information on child trafficking within the region. The road ahead will be difficult. From what I've been told and since read online, it will take a miracle to get Sarah back safely.

Taylor reminded me to keep my strength and determination at the forefront and to never give up hope, but at the same time, I shouldn't get my hopes up.

George helped as much as he could. The US Embassy dispatched a BOLO to all agencies and sent out a media release. The story was picked up, and Sarah's photo has been distributed on all media platforms, listed as a missing person. Seeing her face on the news sites and across social media has been devastating. The image used tells a story of a happier time, one where we baked a cake for Liam's birthday. Although her smiling photo joins the hundreds of other missing children around the world, our story is getting coverage because Sarah is an attractive, young white American girl.

In his own stoic manner, George explained how the investigation with the local authorities would move ahead along with the possible implications of talking to the media. He provided some useful advice on how I could use the media but cautioned me to be very careful as to what I said about the local government and agencies. Apparently, the Emiratis don't take kindly to bad press even if what's being said is true.

Our little crisis headquarters was for dealing with a ransom demand only. Being surrounded by Americans and watching them take the lead with everything on our behalf almost made me forget where we were. With the embassy moving on, it's left me stranded in a void of information inside a home that now seems desolate, hopeless.

Since it wasn't a kidnapping of a US citizen for ransom, the embassy can no longer warrant prioritizing its resources on the case. The abduction's now a missing person case with possible ties to a human-trafficking ring.

In my eyes, she is still high priority.

She's my daughter.

My life.

My world.

Two days, and we don't have any new information. Without the diplomatic buffer provided by the embassy, I've been trying to find out from Lieutenant Ahmed if the police have found any new leads. He said they're investigating, and we'll be informed if they find anything.

Two days, and nothing.

And this is how I've ended up on a deserted beach in Jumeirah, watching the sun go down, a gin and tonic–filled travel mug as my companion. It's against the law to consume alcohol outside a hotel or a private residence. In fact, it's against the law to consume alcohol in your home if you are a UAE resident and don't have a liquor license. It being Ramadan, it's also against the law to eat or drink in public. Tonight, I'm breaking three laws.

It's not unusual for stories of misdemeanors to infiltrate the expat gossip network. In fact, the local paper likes to write about them as a cautionary tale. It's actually a common occurrence for tourists to find out the hard way how strict the liquor laws are and how seriously they're taken. Drinking alcohol in public, being drunk, overt displays of affection, sex outside of marriage—all against the law and offer a one-way ticket to a local jail cell. If it were left to my imagination, I would see them being left in a dark, damp, overcrowded cell, anxiously awaiting trial, only to find out that they'd been forgotten.

I think of my sweet little girl. She's ten. She hasn't committed a crime.

She's the victim.

Now, she's alone somewhere, suffering the consequences of my lack of vigilance. We haven't been updated on the investigation by the Dubai Police. There are, however, two people who might know something, but they're locked away, awaiting trial and, more than likely, deportation.

I begged to talk to the woman who had taken Sarah as well as the Russian man identified as being part of the trafficking ring, but the local authorities said no. I pleaded with the embassy to step in and champion my cause with the Emiratis. They also said no but were much nicer about it. Sympathetic even.

The embassy did divulge that they'd received copies of the interview transcripts from the two prisoners. Although George wouldn't let me read them, he explained the transcripts weren't anything more than statements from both individuals, testifying they had no knowledge of Sarah's whereabouts. The whole situation is infuriating. The local police have members of a human-trafficking ring operating on their sovereign soil, and they can't find out where Sarah is.

I know any investigation into the legal transportation methods will be flawed, as they'll only show documented travel. It's a well-hidden scar to their strict moral standards that minor airstrips within the UAE allow black flights— flights that aren't logged and used by smugglers or worse. A friend's husband was the air traffic controller at Fujairah, and apparently, he was asked to leave the tower on occasion when unregistered or private flights would land or take off. These flights were never logged and completely under the radar from the officials. Or maybe they were done at the behest of other officials for those with *wasta*, or power.

I sip my drink and run my hand through the sand. This sand … this sand is a lie. This is not the sand from a coastal town somewhere on a beach that promises an easy and happy life. I'm sitting not twenty feet from a body of water, but it's not an ocean. It's the Persian Gulf, the conduit that floats the cargoes of oil, which enrich the countries surrounding it and the companies involved in its extraction, refinement, and trade. Oil being nothing more than the remnants of ancient plants and animals representing a life that no longer exists in this barren place. Covered and, until recently, forgotten by desert. This sand is from the desert that represents anything but life. Nothing can grow in the desert. I don't understand how the Emiratis think they can cultivate a city from it. A city from a granule of sand? Everything in this city is a clever mirage. Pretty and shiny but fake.

All that glitters is not gold.

A long shadow moves across the sand toward me, alerting me to another presence on the beach, and pulls me from my melancholy musings. I might no longer be the lone person here, but I'm desperately alone. In my peripheral vision, I watch Melanie approach, and she takes a seat beside me. I ignore her and continue staring at the water. I don't want to acknowledge her because she isn't Kevin, and I really wanted it to be him. I needed it to be him.

"I was at your villa, and Anika told me where I could find you."

I like the way Melanie never asks how I am. She knows. We continue to sit in silence as the heat of the day disappears with the sun. The water mimics my mind with the currents smoothly pulling it away from where it's trying to go. The irony isn't lost on me.

"I needed some fresh air and space to think," I finally say. My voice is quiet, and the words are carried away on the gentle breeze.

"I understand. It must be quiet in the villa with the FBI and embassy staff gone."

"Yes," I agree, raising my cup to my lips. "It's been very quiet. At least when they were there—when we thought it was a kidnapping—we had hope. They kept in close contact with the Dubai Police and passed the information on. I had confidence in the process, and I had an idea of what was going on …"

Melanie softly prods a few minutes after I trailed off. "And, now, you don't?"

"No, I don't. How can I when they won't tell me what's going on? They won't let me question the people they have in custody. When I call, I get the same damn response. *The case is proceeding as planned. If we have anything new of relevance, we'll let you know.* I'm wandering around in a dark tunnel with no beacon of light to lead me out." I swallow a lump in my throat as I attempt to keep the tears that are threatening to fall at bay. "No one knows where Sarah is or who has her. All they can tell me is that she's not in the country anymore. This … this whole situation is ripping my family apart."

"No, it's not." Her soft voice, offering patient understanding, aggravates me.

"It is!" The loud, forceful words ricochet across the deserted beach. Melanie's stillness and tolerance calm something inside me. I repeat the words more quietly. "It is."

Night's fallen, and we're left sitting in the muted light from the street behind us. The Ramadan moon shines high in the sky, and the *muezzin*'s call to prayer echoes through the silence. I wrap my arms around my legs, resting my chin on my knees, wondering what Kevin is doing now.

After our move, we were so infatuated with the region and its hidden secrets. Every time we heard the call to prayer, we'd share a secret smile. We were excited to explore our host country and indulge in its extravagances, both modern and ancient. Until Kevin's work started to require more time from him, time away from us.

"Kevin has hardly been home. He blames me for everything; I know it."

"I'm sure he doesn't."

I shake my head. "No. He does. I see it written plainly on his face as he avoids me. He can't look at me. He won't even talk to me."

"I'm sure he needs time to deal with everything in his own way."

"That's what he said, but I think it's just a stalling tactic. He's angry, Mel. And I can feel all his anger directed toward me. He blames me for everything, and I can't help but feel that he's justified."

"I know you feel guilty about what's happened, but it's not your fault. It's no one's fault but the abductors'. Have you talked to anyone about this?"

"Like who?"

"A grief counselor or the local pastor?"

"You think talking to anyone will make this better? Will help us find Sarah?"

"No, of course not. But they'll help sort through your feelings. Keeping your emotional state tightly under wraps isn't healthy. It's not healthy for Liam. He needs to be able to talk through these things with someone who isn't involved before it turns into something worse. Both you and Kevin are obviously having some issues with coping. You need to deal with this before it festers and one of you does or says something you can't take back. You need to get through this as a family, and a professional counselor can help you work through it. No, it's not going to help you find Sarah, but it will help you sort through everything, so you can deal with the important things—like what you need to do to find her. You need to be at your healthiest to tackle what's to come." Melanie takes my travel mug and dumps it onto the sand. It's empty, but the gesture is meant to be symbolic. "You need to be at your healthiest, both physically and mentally."

I sigh and hug my knees, focusing on the dark water. "I'll think about it."

13

____

My heart's hurting, but I'm determined not to lose hope. It's been a week since Sarah's abduction, and still, nothing. Things between Kevin and me have remained tense, which hasn't made our situation any easier. He's hardly around, and when he is, he doesn't want to discuss counseling. A cloud of tension hangs over the villa, and its intensity doesn't dissipate when he's gone. When he's home, we basically share information from the day and update each other on what we might have found out from either the embassy or the police, which really has been nothing.

George, in his capacity as the US Embassy's regional security officer, or RSO, sent out a media release on the disappearance of a US national. Various international news platforms picked up the story, and the embassy has been bombarded with questions and requests for more information. Instead of answering the individual media agency's questions, George suggested a press conference, and we've been asked to attend.

Kevin's against the idea of being involved. He doesn't want his face plied across televisions, newspapers, or magazines. He's also concerned with how this will be perceived by the UAE government and officials. He believes it will affect him in a professional capacity—as if that's an important factor right now. It took a bit of convincing, but I got him to agree.

We're parked outside the new US Consulate on al-Seef Road in Bur Dubai. The embassy staff decided to hold the press conference here instead of in the embassy building in Abu Dhabi. Before Kevin turns the engine off for us to step out into the humid morning, we share a moment of uncomfortable silence. Kevin white-knuckles the steering wheel and holds his back rigid against the seat. He's frustrated at being here, but he's equally concerned about what it'll look like if he isn't by my side when I make my emotional plea to the world to help find our daughter.

"This is a bad idea, Jen. Are you sure you want to do this?" Kevin asks, hoping I'll change my mind.

"No, it's not, and yes, we need to be here. There needs to be a face to Sarah's abduction. If we have the media's support, someone might come forward with information that'll help find her," I repeat for what feels like the hundredth time.

Kevin shakes his head and stares out the window, watching the increasing morning traffic. "The Dubai Police aren't going to be happy about this. They don't like their shortcomings being on display for the world to see."

"This has nothing to do with the Dubai Police. The embassy's already sent a press release, and we're here to be the face of that."

Kevin grunts with annoyance, and I can't help the growl of frustration erupting, so I quickly cover it up by pretending to clear my throat. It's been like this all week. His passive-aggressiveness is a constant reminder of our growing distance.

I continue more softly in an attempt to appease him. "It's why we're here, Kevin. Doing it with the embassy. They'll control the narrative and make sure nothing's said to jeopardize the police investigation. George said he already talked to Lieutenant Ahmed and will brief us before we face the reporters."

A rap on the car window startles me, and a face peers at us through the tint. Kevin hits the button and lowers the glass a fraction, letting in the morning humidity.

A peppy voice addresses us. "Mrs. Johnson? Mr. Johnson?"

"Yes?"

"Ah, great. Mr. Bailey sent me out to escort you. He didn't want you arriving via the main entrance. The media is already on-site, and we didn't want to risk an ambush before the press conference."

"Okay," I say, unbuckling my seat belt. "We need to do this, Kevin. For Sarah," I say quietly.

Kevin has yet to move. I turn toward him, taking in the fixed set of his jaw, his eyes staring straight ahead, and his hands still firmly gripping the steering wheel.

Kevin slowly nods and reluctantly climbs from the car.

"Just follow me, please." Again with the peppiness.

We're taken into the building through a maze of secured doors. Finally, Ms. Peppy leads us into a small conference room within the consulate and asks us to wait. The aroma of fresh coffee has me in the corner, grabbing a cup. Kevin sits and plays with his phone. I wonder if we were meant to leave our phones in the car or declare them before entering the building. A camera subtly placed in the far corner of the ceiling will undoubtedly alert someone to our faux pas if this is the case.

I'm filling my second cup of coffee when George walks in, a file under his arm, holding a lockbox. One of his assistants is standing in the doorway, waiting expectantly.

"Good to see you both," he says, shaking our hands with familiarity. "How are you holding up?"

"We're holding," I say on a sigh.

He nods a knowing response. "Okay, I wanted to take a few minutes to run through the sequence of events and talk about how best to answer any questions directed to you. But, first, I'll need to secure your phones and any other electronic devices you might have. We'll return them before you leave." He unlocks the box and expectantly holds his hand out for Kevin's phone.

I pull mine out of my bag and hand it over. George secures the phones and turns to hand the box off to his assistant, who scurries away.

"Thank you. As you're aware, the UAE government isn't big on press conferences, especially in circumstances like this where there's the potential to show them in a poor light. This needs to be handled with discretion."

"Exactly my concern," Kevin says. He nods and turns to me with a look of vindication. "I can't afford to ruffle any feathers with the Emiratis. As much as I want to get the word out there about Sarah, I can't do it at the expense of our family's security and well-being."

"I totally understand, and that's why we're here to help guide you through this. We'll be doing this in our pressroom, which is down two levels from where we are now. The reporters will already be seated in the room before we arrive. We'll enter from a side door and position ourselves on the dais behind the lectern. The consul general and I will accompany you onto the dais, and we'll start the briefing. He or I will review the facts of the disappearance—nothing more than what was sent out in the press release and BOLO—and then we'll introduce you. You'll have the opportunity to make a plea for the public to come forward if they have pertinent information. After that, I'll open the floor to questions. Make sense?"

"Who are people meant to contact if they know something?" I ask, fidgeting with the handle on my coffee cup. I'm suddenly nervous about not knowing the answers to any questions.

George smiles, opens his folder, and pulls out a sheet of paper. "We've prepared this statement. They each received a copy when they arrived. It has all of that information on it. I'll field any questions related to the ongoing investigation, so you won't have to worry about that either."

"Good. This is good," Kevin says, reading over the statement, nodding. He appears more relaxed now that George has said the embassy will field most of the questions.

"Don't worry; everything will be fine. I know it goes without saying, but we do need to be careful not to discuss anything that'll impact the police investigation. I've been over our briefing points with Lieutenant Ahmed, and he's happy as long as we stick to the script."

"Exactly what can we say?" Kevin asks.

George sighs. "We can say the police are looking into Sarah's disappearance and the investigation is ongoing."

"That's it?" I ask incredulously.

"Yes," George answers. "It's probably easier to discuss what we can't talk about. We can't mention the police have people in custody. Or the possible links to the Russian Mafia or human trafficking."

"What are we meant to say when people ask us what's going on? I'm assuming the Dubai Police don't want us talking about this to anyone, not only the press?" Kevin asks, concern etched on his face.

He's worried about upsetting the UAE government. He's right to be concerned. The UAE has strict censorship laws. Anyone caught damaging the reputation of Dubai or the UAE government or talking out against the royal family or officials in any of the seven emirates faces arrest. Freedom of speech is nonexistent, and the restrictions are reinforced with reminders at every cinema visit to watch a movie with deleted scenes or every bought magazine with body parts blacked out with a Sharpie.

"You can say anything that's already been sent out in the previous press release. And, of course, anything said today. For today's briefing, I wouldn't stray far from the facts that your daughter went missing from the Mall of the

Emirates and that the police are investigating. We can mention she's likely been taken out of the country, and there's no indication of Emirati nationals being involved. You can also mention you've been working closely with the local authorities and you're very happy with how they're dealing with the situation."

"So, we can lie?" I'm not too sure if I'm happy with how the police are dealing with the situation. I still haven't heard whether the two people they have in custody have provided any actionable information on Sarah's location.

"Lie about what?" George asks, perplexed.

"That we're working closely with the police and we're happy with how they're dealing with the situation ..." I trail off when Kevin frowns. "What? I'm not happy with not knowing anything."

"Well, the first part isn't really a lie," George says, scratching his head as he watches both Kevin and me. "We were in constant contact with the police during those initial forty-eight hours when it was thought to be a kidnapping case. We also receive weekly updates on all open cases pertaining to US citizens, and Sarah's disappearance is included in those briefings. To be honest, you should be happy with how seriously they've dealt with this situation. A variety of cases cross our desk, and you're fortunate to have Lieutenant Ahmed spearheading this investigation. He's been as transparent as they can be."

I understand policing here is different from back home, and I know we're fortunate they've been both supportive and proactive from the beginning. It just kills me that we don't know anything, and as far as I know, all their leads have gone nowhere. It's so goddamn infuriating.

I push my coffee cup away from me on the table and scoot back in my chair. Something has been grating on my nerves this morning, and I want George to explain it to me. "You've said the word *disappearance* a few times now. Is that what we're meant to be calling Sarah's abduction?

Why can't we call it what it is? She hasn't disappeared; she was taken. They targeted her and stole her. Abducted her. Any of those words work better for what we know happened. Why are you calling it a *disappearance*?"

George exhales loudly and rubs his forehead while he rocks back on his chair. I've seen him do this repeatedly over the past week; it's his tell. He's frustrated, and I can't blame him. I can't begin to understand the political tightrope he must walk daily. Regardless, I've had enough of it, and I'm only trying to find out where my daughter is.

"Mrs. Johnson, your daughter's been registered as a missing person. Unfortunately, it's the way we need to play it to maintain political support from the Emiratis. There's a fine line for what can be said and not said. It's important you don't mention the words *stolen*, *taken*, or *abducted*. We don't want to alienate you from your current host government."

"Can we ask for local support?"

George scrunches his face up in thought. It's a valid question because Sarah's abduction hasn't aired on any local news. It's been picked up by the BBC and CNN and even Al Jazeera, but nothing has been shown on City 7 or Dubai One, and nothing has made it to the local or regional newspapers.

"Yes. You can appeal to anybody who thinks they might have seen anything or who knows anything to please contact their local police or Interpol. The news stations will provide the relevant contact details. But, yes, you definitely can make that appeal."

"What questions should we expect?" Kevin asks.

I swivel in my chair to face George as he answers. "First of all, if they ask anything you don't want to answer, just look at me, and I'll either answer on your behalf or redirect them. As I said, we'll answer anything to do with the investigation or political relations. To be honest, they'll probably just want to focus on Sarah—who she was as a person, her hobbies and interests, whether she was a good student. That sort of thing." He pauses and starts fidgeting with the briefing folder in front of him. Looking back up at us, he continues. "This is a good thing. If we can turn Sarah into a real person, people will have an interest in helping."

My mouth opens, but it takes a few seconds before I whisper the words out. "She *is* a real person."

George looks down, red flushing his cheeks. "Yes, sorry. Probably not the best way to express what I meant. There are thousands of missing children reports open. To gain coverage, you need audience support or interest. That's done when you pull the heartstrings, when you connect with the viewers. By talking about your family life and Sarah's interests, you are creating that connection with the viewer or the reader. Watching this, people need to have a reason to remember, to have it in the backs of their minds in the event they see or hear something. It gives them more of an incentive to help."

Kevin and I nod in understanding. It makes me sick, thinking of all the children who are in the same position as Sarah, that there are so many missing. I hope and pray the Dubai Police are doing everything to shut this child-trafficking ring—if that's what it is—down for good. If talking about Sarah to the press can help achieve that in any way, I'm ready to help. These predators need to be stopped.

The door opens, and Ambassador Sullivan walks in. We've met once before when he came to the house to check in on the first day Sarah went missing and offered his condolences. He does the same now.

"Hello, Ambassador," Kevin says as he stands and shakes hands with him. "Are you joining us for the press conference this morning?"

The ambassador smiles a greeting in my direction and returns his focus to Kevin as he adjusts his cuffs. "No, Mr. Johnson. George will be heading this on our behalf, and the consul general will be in attendance." As he pulls down on his cuffs, he sees the confusion on our faces. His hands move up to adjust the silk tie that sets off his expensive suit. "I came in to pass on my regards and wish you luck. Also, to remind you that we're walking a fine political line here in the UAE. The United States has enjoyed good relations with the UAE since 1971. Did you know we were only the third country to establish formal diplomatic relations with the Emiratis?"

I shake my head, momentarily lost to where he's going with the impromptu history lesson.

Kevin answers, "Yes, sir."

The ambassador continues, "We all know what's going on here and where the local investigation is. We know they've apprehended people who appear to operate a human-trafficking ring. This is serious, and we can't jeopardize their investigation into this in any way. I realize your daughter has fallen victim, but our hands are tied as to how much diplomatic pressure we can exert on them to get a resolution. Their laws and ideas of human rights are a lot different than what we're used to back in the States. We might fault the methods they have used or might use, but they're working within their legal framework. Do you understand?"

"Yes, sir. But—" Kevin starts.

"Good," the ambassador cuts in, and he looks at his watch. He steps around George's vacated chair to shake my hand and then shakes Kevin's. "It's important you stick to the facts as briefed to you by the RSO and let him or the CG field any questions regarding the investigation. Good luck."

The ambassador gives George a quick nod and exits the room. If I'd blinked, I might have missed it.

"Okay, where were we?" George asks, picking up his notes once again.

"No talking about the investigation. Only answer questions we feel comfortable with regarding Sarah and our life," I reply desolately.

All the hope and enthusiasm I had on entering the building, thinking we could use the press conference to create dialogue and awareness, has disappeared. I knew we'd be restricted in what we could say to the press, but it's like someone just took a Sharpie and censored my whole being. It's not fair, and what's worse, Sarah's going to pay for it.

"Yes. Are you ready to do this?" George says, finding no humor in my grim reply.

"Yes. Let's get this over with," Kevin says.

At least he appears happier to be here.

———

We follow George, and I can't help but note how Kevin's demeanor and mine have switched so abruptly within the last few minutes. He's not as sullen and angry while I've lost my motivation and hope. He's even making small talk with the consul general, who's joined our procession to the pressroom.

Noise echoing along the corridor alerts us to the pressroom before we reach it. We come to a halt before doors that open into a large briefing room. Loud discussion and laughing are heard from within. In front of the podium are rows of chairs with blue leather cushioning. The assistant who escorted us into the building quickly opens the door and steps through. The noise dies immediately, and in the brief moment the door is ajar, I can see the podium with an American flag standing on each side of it.

"Are you ready to do this?" George repeats his words from the conference room. He adjusts his posture, and a change washes over him as he switches into professional mode.

I slightly tilt my head in assent. I take Kevin's hand and give it a quick squeeze. He looks to me and offers a small smile. I'll take it. And, as though we rehearsed this, we walk through the doors and stand next to the podium, beside the CG and George.

The room erupts almost straightaway. The din seems to magnify as camera flashes leave spots behind my eyes and blur my vision. I tighten my grip on Kevin's hand, swallowing uneasily while I watch the people in front of me. Sweat beads above my brow, generated by the bright lights focused on the dais.

"Calm down, people. Calm down. You know how this is done. Let's keep it together, please. Now ..." George takes control of the room and starts the briefing.

I listen, but I don't hear the words. I know what he's going to say. As George talks, I look straight ahead, staring at nothing. Tears well up, unasked, as I think about Sarah. It's been over a week, and I wish we could do more than just stand here and talk about what a good daughter, student, and friend she was—*is*.

I'm in a trance, floating above my body, watching the proceedings from afar. My timid and hesitant statements are in complete contrast with the bravado and enthusiasm I had only a few hours ago.

Will Sarah see this? Will she see how worried we are for her, how much we miss her? And how much we love her?

I wonder if she'll see how much I need her. Because I do. There's a hole in my heart, and she's the only one who can fill it. I hope she'll be able to see all of my emotions despite these hot, bright lights.

14

The return drive to the villa after leaving the consulate was solemn. Both Kevin and I were lost in our own reverie.

My thoughts are with Sarah. Some of the questions the press asked has my mind wandering down a darkened path.

One of the reporters had flown in from London and was linked to Human Rights Watch, if the note she slipped to me after the press conference is any indication. I've heard of HRW before. I've even read some of their stories on the labor camps outside Dubai that house those poor souls who build Dubai for a pittance. I don't know how she was granted an entry visa. Normally, the Emiratis are extremely vigilant in not allowing activists to enter the country.

I'm not sure whether she was reporting on behalf of the newspaper she said she represented or was looking into this on behalf of HRW; it was hard to tell. What I do know is that HRW is a dirty word in the UAE due to their reporting on serious human rights problems that they say are being masked by the overt wealth. Things like freedom of speech, mistreatment of construction workers, and house help. I cringe, thinking about the rumored people accused of criticizing the government and being investigated by the Emiratis. I hope to never find out if there's any truth to those tales.

"I won't be home tonight. I've a late meeting, and then I'm flying to Kuwait to meet with the adviser from Risk Management Corps. Tell Liam I'll call him in the morning," Kevin says, bringing me out of my thoughts.

We're parked out front of the villa, and his words, meant to be my dismissal, have me turning to him in surprise.

"What? Why are you meeting with RMC? You already said they wouldn't be able to help; they don't investigate. I thought that's what George told you as well."

From what I was told, RMC is one of many private security firms operating in the Middle East and North Africa, which had cropped up in the wake of 9/11 and the US invasions of Afghanistan and Iraq, with a lot of elite military servicemen cashing in their uniforms and dog tags for an exorbitant monthly paycheck. They are effectively business corporations that provide armed and unarmed security services and information to any paying client. Kevin's company occasionally contracts their security out to them if they are traveling into a city like Baghdad, Kirkuk, or Kabul. Even though a lot of private security companies have a bad reputation for being paid mercenaries, I'm thankful they exist and have operators trained in high-risk situations, just in case. But Kevin seeking one out when we've already been advised not to by the embassy's security staff is asking for trouble.

Kevin drums his fingers on the steering wheel, like my question irritates him. "Yes, I realize that, but I want to make sure we've covered all our bases. There's something out there that we're missing. Maybe, just maybe, they can find that something. I want to understand what my options are."

"Don't you think that's a risk? You heard what the ambassador said, what we've been told from the beginning; we can't openly talk about what's really going on with the investigation or Sarah's abduction."

Kevin's hands still, and he turns to look at me. "I know that, Jen. But I know the operations officer for the company, and I'm sure he'll keep our confidences. They have to be informed of the situation; otherwise, how can they advise me?"

I nod slowly in response. He's right; we do need to make sure we're doing everything possible. If Sarah's not in the UAE, we might be able to do *something* to track her down without upsetting their domestic investigation.

Kevin's jaw tightens as his eyes lose a bit of their warmth. "I'm also looking into obtaining outside legal counsel to work out what options we have here in Dubai."

"What for?" I ask with an uncertain tone as my stomach flutters. My mind races, trying to work out why we would need legal counsel.

"Just in case."

"Just in case of what?" I quickly shoot back, the panic bubbling up.

"Jesus. Do I need a reason? Let's pick one, why don't we? How about if the government puts a freeze on our accounts or if we're asked to leave? Or what about if we're accused of doing something we didn't? Does it really matter?" Kevin is all but shouting at me.

"Oh my God. Quit it with the attitude already. I only asked why. Don't you think you should've brought this up with me earlier?" I snap.

Kevin's anger is getting old fast, and it hurts more than I'd like to believe. It's hard, realizing our relationship only started spiraling not long after our move to the Middle East. New money and prestige were seemingly the catalysts for our increasing issues. Not for the first time, I lament our life in Virginia.

"No. I'm too busy to run my every thought past you." He scrubs his hand over his face. "I'm just looking at options and making sure we're protected. Listen, I don't have time for this now. I have to get to the office."

"Okay," I concede. "So, you're in Kuwait tonight. Will you be home tomorrow? We need to sit down and talk," I say gently. I really don't know how he's continued to work through all of this. The stress of it all must be eating him away from the inside.

"I don't know. Maybe. I'll let you know," he says through a sigh, placing the car in drive.

It's my cue to get out. I lean over and give him a peck on the cheek before turning to open the car door. I try not to take it to heart that he didn't lean into my affection. I also try to not let it bother me that what he said was a lie. He won't let me know. I'll just have to work it out myself and keep the remainder of the family unit moving forward.

15

———

"Jen? Are you home?"

I grimace at the voices coming from the front foyer. A few of my friends invited themselves around to my villa for a coffee morning. I haven't seen them since we caught up at the Lime Tree Café the morning of Sarah's abduction, and I've successfully avoided them, both on the phone and at school drop-offs. Until now. Thankfully, I had a heads-up of their intentions via text message from Melanie. The timing for their visit couldn't be worse.

Since the press conference a few days ago, it's been frustrating, leaving home. A few reporters have been following me around, trying to persuade me to give an exclusive interview. Our story is now global, and as a result, I've been inundated with calls. Some have been from family and friends stateside, calling to offer a sympathetic ear or, in the majority of cases, trying to get the *real story*.

When most people see or hear the words *Middle East*, they believe there's more to the story. As though everything from this region is related to some sort of conspiracy, whether it be political or terrorism. It's as though we've been conditioned to think nothing good can come out of the Middle East. Admittedly, I thought the same thing until we moved to the region and were able to engage the people and see some of the wonders of Arabia. But, now, with everything that's going on, I'm not too sure.

The hounding reporters and nosy friends want the real story, but my hands are tied. I can't tell them what's really going on. To do so could jeopardize our visa, Kevin's work, and of course, the ongoing police investigation. It could also, and more importantly, jeopardize Sarah's safety, and I would never do that.

"In the kitchen," I call, switching the kettle on to heat water for coffee. As I turn, I'm embraced by arms and pulled into a group hug.

"Jen."

"Oh my God, any word?"

"Monica, Kate," I say, untangling myself from their arms. I smile at Melanie over their shoulders as she shrugs and mouths a silent apology. "It's nice of you to stop by."

"We brought wine." Monica, ever the lush, pulls a bottle out of her oversize designer handbag with a flourish. Get-togethers with expat wives normally involve alcohol.

"And food," Kate says, retrieving a brown paper bag she discarded on the hall table. She hesitates but smiles before handing it to me. "On the way over, I stopped by Lime Tree to pick up some sandwiches and cake."

I return her smile with a small one of my own. I hoped the company might take my mind off the investigation and the lack of information from the police, but I'm not too sure now that they're here, in my space. It might have been worth the risk, braving the outside world and agreeing to meet at a hotel café. At least then, I could have left if I wanted to, and with the media and police attention, I would've had a plausible excuse to do so.

The pop as the cork exits the bottle is muted by the flurry of questions coming hard and fast from both Kate and Monica. I ignore them until we're in the back sitting room, by the pool.

"Do you know there's a police car parked a few houses up?" Kate asks, taking a seat and holding her hand out for a glass. "He actually got out and walked down this way when I parked in front of your villa."

Monica groans, and her glossed lips pucker up into her version of a grimace. "Yeah, tell me about it. I was about to walk in with the wine in my hand. I saw him just in time to hide the bottle in my bag. So, are they out there, watching for kidnappers or something?"

Kate sits forward in her seat, fingers playing with the stem of the wineglass. "Have there been any updates?"

"I read the article CNN put out. They spoke about other disappearances in the region and how they were related to the child sex trade. Is that what they're thinking?" Monica blurts out before I can answer the previous question.

I take a seat and study my friends. Monica and Kate are sitting on the edge of their seats, waiting expectantly. Both women are dressed as though they were attending a Friday champagne brunch—pretty summer dresses with wedge heels, perfectly manicured nails, and professionally applied makeup. Melanie, in contrast, sits back in her chair, and appears comfortable in her yoga pants and oversize T-shirt, silently shaking her head.

I'm concerned with how much I can tell them. Melanie knows pretty much everything, but I trust her to hold my confidence. The danger lies with the other two—Monica more so than Kate. Anything I say here will be repeated and submitted into the expat wives' gossip network.

"No. There hasn't been any more information. The police are still investigating," I say, keeping with the standard response.

My eyes briefly meet Melanie's, and she gives me a subtle nod, letting me know she understands.

"The police outside ..." Kate queries, arching a perfectly manicured eyebrow.

"I've been hassled by a few reporters who want follow-up interviews after our press conference at the consulate. The police are there as a deterrent to keep the harassment to a minimum. I'm not sure who gave the hacks our address and phone numbers, but they've become quite insistent." I take a sip of the wine. Its crisp flavor awakens my palate. I was never a big drinker until Sarah's disappearance. Now, there isn't a day I'm strong enough to shut it all off and catch some sleep without a drink in my hand.

"Are you going to talk to them? The reporters, I mean," Monica asks.

I smile sadly. "No. I have nothing to say to them. Everything I could say or would say has already been said. And, to be honest, I don't really want to keep repeating the same sentiments or giving in to their speculation."

"Could say? Well, you could start by telling the truth that Sarah was abducted from the mall rather than just disappearing," Monica snaps. Her eyes don't leave mine as both Kate and Melanie gasp in astonishment. "The speculation is fair on their part. You obviously know more about what's going on; otherwise, you'd be jumping up and down, demanding answers and getting all emotional over the worst-case scenarios that everyone's whispering about."

My face heats as I glare into the eyes of my friend. Monica has always been a bit of a bitch, but I never thought she could be this cruel.

"You caught me, Monica. Aren't you the clever one? I do know a bit more, but I'm not at liberty to discuss it with them or anyone else for that matter. My daughter's life is at stake here. I've also done more than enough of my own speculation as to where Sarah is and what's happening." My words come out a bit too loud and forceful. I take a deep breath and continue in a slightly calmer tone. "I can't afford to let my emotions control me. With everything going on, there's just too much at stake.

It's not just Sarah. Her disappearance has affected everyone in the house." My words trail off, and I turn away from the group. I don't want to be here, having this discussion.

I fathom, as mothers, their desire for information, but I hoped they'd have more compassion for what I'm going through.

Ignoring my words and unspoken plea to let it drop, Monica continues. "Her disappearance has affected more than that. There's heightened security at the school, at the malls. It's affecting us all because we don't know whether there's a kidnapping ring, a child porn ring, or a terrorist cell at work here. We could all be at risk."

Of course, my daughter being taken would be all about her. I understand her frustration, anger, and fear, I do, but I just don't want to weigh in on all the speculation. Those thoughts cross my mind daily, and having her feed into it could send me spiraling into a dark place. As it is, I'm holding on to my sanity by a thread. Sarah's abduction, Liam's withdrawal, and the strain everything is putting on my marriage. If I let it, it would all take me down. Feed my anxieties. It would break me.

"Monica, I think that's enough," Melanie says quietly.

I look to Kate, but her attention is on Monica, nodding in agreement. I now understand Kate's initial hesitation when she arrived. This wasn't necessarily a social visit or a visit to offer their support. They planned on coming here to interrogate me. On one hand, I understand their concern. In their minds, their children are potentially at risk. In reality, they probably are, but the risk hasn't risen because my daughter was abducted. If anything, it has lessened with the police moving in on the perpetrators.

"If you told the truth, people would know and could make their own informed decision if it was safe to remain living here. I mean, to be honest, look at you. You're holed up here, in the villa, while your husband ..." Monica says softly before she trails off. She averts her eyes and stares out the window at the pool.

"What about Kevin?" I'm confused. I don't understand the question.

Kevin has been working. He goes to the office, attends his meetings, and does his work. Admittedly, it'd be nice if he took time off to be here for Liam and me. But he's following the advice given to us by the embassy and security specialists. I almost wish I had something to do during the day to distract my mind.

Monica shakes her head and adds a wry laugh. I glance over to Kate and Melanie, but they look as perplexed as I feel.

"What about Kevin?" Monica says, mimicking my words. "What does he think about all of this?"

"He's just as devastated as I am. And frustrated. You know this," I reply carefully.

I assumed Kevin had been confiding in her husband, David, and spending the time out of our villa with him. That, if David was in the know, Monica was to a degree as well.

"Would I? And what do you mean by that?" Monica asks dryly.

"Well, if it's office gossip, you'd know, wouldn't you? I'm surprised you're not complaining about him spending more time drinking with David or crashing on your couch."

Monica pauses a moment, giving me a strange look, which flitters over her face before she laughs and shakes her head with pity. "So, you're going to lie about that as well?"

"What do you mean?" I ask, suddenly realizing I don't know what we're talking about anymore.

Monica laughs quietly, giving me another weird look before pursing her lips. She opens her mouth to say something but shakes her head again instead. I've had enough of whatever is going on and her holier-than-thou accusatory attitude.

Before she can gather her thoughts and answer my question, I continue. "Don't worry about it. I'm sure you know best; you always do. Always butting in on everyone's business and playing office politics. Forever needing to be the queen bee. Well, you can run back to your husband now and give him your updated report. I think I'm done here."

I stand and start gathering up the glasses and uneaten food from the coffee table, my movements jerky and rushed. I've enough on my plate to deal with, and I don't need pressure and derision put on me by my so-called friends.

Monica approaches and gently places her hands on my shoulders. "I'm sorry. Maybe I was out of line. Obviously, there's a lot going on, and I can't imagine what it feels like, trying to deal with it all. I'm sure you'd tell us more if you could, and I'm sorry if I suggested otherwise. I think I should go. We can catch up another time." She releases my shoulders and walks over to the couch she was sitting on to collect her handbag. With a small smile to the other girls, she leaves the room.

We stay motionless, listening to her heels click across the tiled floor as she heads down the hallway to the front door. The noisy bang as the door closes signals her exit from the villa.

"Well ..." I start to say but trail off when I see Kate and Melanie staring at me, flabbergasted. "What?"

"It's not like you to get all bitchy. You were all up in her face," Kate says.

"No, I wasn't," I say defensively. "And even if I were, don't you think I have that right? It's my daughter who's missing. My family who's suffering. None of you know or understand."

"I think the bitch status belongs completely to Monica," Melanie mutters as I leave the room, retreating to the kitchen.

I take a seat on a kitchen stool and scrub my face before leaning forward to rest my chin in my hands. I'm ashamed of my words, but I'm just too tired to care enough to do anything about it. I'm on edge, and I don't think I deserve to be spoken to like that. After all, my life is falling in ruins around me, and my daughter's missing. If anyone needs an apology, it should be me. But I can't afford to push people away.

Forlorn, I look up and offer a small smile as Kate enters the kitchen, Melanie behind her. I reluctantly stand as Kate comes over for a hug.

"It'll be okay. Everything will be okay. I'm sure they'll find Sarah soon," she whispers before ending the hug. "I'd better go, too. Let me know if there is any news." With a final wave, Kate leaves.

"So ..." Melanie says.

I burst out laughing. I can't help it. Shaking my head, I sit back down, the laughter quickly turning into sobs. My emotions are all over the place. I take in a deep breath and let it out with a whoosh. "Yes, that quickly spiraled out of hand. Why is everyone in this place so self-centered or fake?"

"Have you contacted the grief counselor yet?" Melanie asks, sitting next to me.

I take in Melanie's kind eyes, thankful to see no judgment or pity. "Yes, but only for Liam. I'm still working on Kevin to see if he'll come with me."

"That's good. You could still go without him, you know. It'll help you deal with the emotions you're keeping bottled up inside."

"I know."

I need to get Kevin home and talk to him to see where his head is. We're still a family, and we should be working through these things together. We need to work out a way forward. There's so much to discuss, but there's also so much distance.

With a grim smile, I stand to start tidying up.

"I know," I whisper again.

16

———

"Mom, why are the police following us?" Liam asks, looking at the reflection in the passenger mirror.

"There've been a few reporters around, trying to talk with us. I think the police are just making sure they're not harassing us. Nothing to worry about."

I reach across the center console and take his hand in mine. He pulls his away and subtly moves his body closer to the door while returning his focus to the cell phone in his other hand. I try not to take it to heart and give him a small smile as I return my hand to the steering wheel.

The week following the press conference and the abortive get-together with my friends was overly stressful. Kevin's notably absent, so much so that Anika asked if he was still living here. She was rather chagrined and cowered away with the response and dirty look I shot her way.

The worst thing about the past week was the story of Sarah's abduction had gone viral. It continues to headline the news back in the US. I know I wanted to get the story out there with the hope that, if anybody had seen something or knew something, they would step forward and we could be one step closer to finding Sarah, but it hasn't happened. What's happened is that right-wing politicians have been using the story to gain political momentum. Trying to sell conspiracies to the West about human trafficking, kidnapping, and child porn rings, all wrapped with a nice dose of how the Middle East is continually in violation of human rights laws. Basically, publicly airing all of the fears Monica raised the other day and adding weight to them.

There've also been media reports lashing out at our parenting. They're claiming we put our children's lives at risk by moving here. None of the reports have come out and said it's our fault directly, but they're implying it. I don't understand how people could say such a thing; we're living in Dubai, not a war-torn country like Iraq or Syria. Our current situation aside, the UAE is one of the safest places to visit with almost a zero crime rate. It's clean and easy to navigate, and it has outstanding schooling and medical facilities. It's just a bit of a joke that news outlets in the US are trying to claim that we're living in a third-world environment.

I know all of this not because we've been able to see or read it in the news here, but because of the multitude of calls I've received from family and friends who are worried about Sarah and our safety. It's amazing, the number of people who have suddenly felt the urge to call and reconnect after years of being absent from our lives. Of course, they all sympathize with our situation and are praying for Sarah's safe return, but they're also quick to weigh in on the political hype happening back in the US, suggesting we should've expected something like this.

My solution has been to stop answering my phone. I wish it were as easy to deal with the reporters stalking me when I'm out. It's not the overt, over-the-top paparazzi with reporters barricading me in the house or chasing me in cars or anything like that. With the laws in place and the sensitivity the government has with the investigation, it's been far subtler. They try to approach me when I'm out doing mundane things, like buying groceries, as though making small talk over a loaf of bread will get me talking about the investigation. It's not as though they go unnoticed either. Lieutenant Ahmed has paid me a visit at home to remind me not to engage with any of them.

I pull up in front of the south gate at Liam's school and wait as he undoes his seat belt and starts rifling through his bag. His hair falls forward, obscuring his face from me.

"Do you have any plans after school today, or do you want me to pick you up at the normal time?"

"No. I've got a group assignment due, and we're staying after school to finish it." He zips the bag and runs his hand over his hair, pushing it back from his face. We really need to get it trimmed. "Is Dad going to be home today?"

I study my son. He's twelve, soon to be thirteen. Still a child yet rapidly becoming a man. It shows in how he's dealing with the situation. At times, he shows such strength, maturity, and understanding beyond his years; it's easy to forget that he's so young. Too young to have to deal with any of it.

"He'll try, buddy. I know he wants to be home with you. He's just busy with work right now."

He shakes his head and exhales loudly. We're both feeling Kevin's absence, and we're both complicit in the lies we're telling ourselves.

"Okay. I'll text when we're done with our work and I'm ready to come home," Liam says with his gaze focused on the school entrance.

It's the peak time of the morning for school drop-off, and a constant stream of kids walk through the gate.

With a shrug, Liam lifts the strap of his bag over his shoulder and turns to me. "Love you, Mom. See you this afternoon."

I watch him with tears in my eyes until he's safely inside the compound before putting the car into gear and driving off.

Coffee. I need coffee. I decide to stop off at the Lime Tree Café to grab a caffeine fix and maybe some carrot cake for Liam's dessert tonight. He loves the café's carrot cake, and I'll use what I can to make him smile and feel loved.

———

I pull into the Spinney parking lot next to the Lime Tree Café and switch off the engine. It feels surreal. The last time I was here was only a few short weeks ago when my only worries were dry cleaning, mail, and making sure my hair and makeup looked good.

We missed the end of Ramadan—or the *Eid al-Fitr* celebrations—when we were holed up, waiting for the ransom call that never came. While the Muslim world celebrated their most joyous days of the Islamic year, we were caught up in a nightmare. One we've yet to wake from.

A knock on my window pulls me into the present and the heat. It doesn't take long for its oppressiveness to work its way inside and turn the car into a sauna. A Pakistani dressed in his *shalwar kameez* lifts a bucket and dirty rag up, silently asking if I want my car washed. I shake my head, grab my purse, and get out of the car.

"Car wash, madam? Twenty dirhams," he asks, trying to convince me. "I clean it very good while you in Spinney's, shopping your groceries."

"Not today, thanks. I'm not going to be here long enough for a car wash."

"I wash it for you fast, madam. I ..." He trails off as a police car drives up behind us.

The car window winds down, and as it slowly passes us, the occupant speaks to the car washer in Arabic. I don't understand what is said, but he looks chastised, cowers, and starts backing away from me.

"Sorry, madam."

"Not a problem," I say, walking toward the café. It's too hot to be outside.

I wish I could see my police shadow as a positive, but it's more intimidating than helpful. For both me and those who cross my path.

17

———

Time stands still when I enter the café. It could be any day of any week or year for that matter. In all the time I've lived in Dubai, the Lime Tree Café on Jumeirah Beach Road has been the one constant. Saliva fills my mouth when I look at the fresh salads and sandwiches in the display case while I wait in line to order. Arugula and roasted pumpkin have never looked so good when paired together.

"What would you like today?" the lady behind the cash register asks with a large smile.

That's the other thing I love about Lime Tree. They've not bowed to the pressure of hiring cheap labor. The staff who work in their cafés have a lot in common, like their love for good food and coffee as well as having English as their first language. It's the simplest things that usually would make me happy, like ordering without having the language barrier, forcing you to repeat your order five times. The large Smartie cookies beside the cash register still the smile on my face as I picture Sarah eating one, dunking it in her hot cocoa.

"I'll have a latte and two pieces of carrot cake—to go, please." Movement in my peripheral vision turns my attention to a free table next to the front window, and I make a snap decision. "You know what? I think I'll drink it here. Can I have my latte and a lemon-roasted chicken on Turkish bread—for here, please? I'll still take the carrot cakes to go."

"Not a problem. One latte and a chicken on Turkish to have here and two carrot cakes to go. That'll be one hundred and eighteen dirhams please." She processes my credit card and hands me a number for my table. "Here you go. Your order will be out soon."

"Thanks." I grab a copy of the newspaper and a few trashy British magazines and head to the vacant table.

The window acts as a barrier between me and the outside world. Beyond the café's tranquil front garden is the busy beach road. I briefly close my eyes and bask in the warmth of the sunshine coming through the dark glaze as it negates the chill of the air-conditioning. If it wasn't for the humidity, Dubai would be perfect. I shudder at the thought. Dubai could never be perfect for me, not with everything that's going on. Not with Sarah still missing.

As reality sets in, I open my eyes and take a deep breath. I unlock the screen on my cell phone. No missed messages and no new emails. I open my email browser and click on the note I received from George at the embassy last night, relaying the latest updates from both Interpol and the Dubai Police. No new information to pass on.

Damn it.

With all the surveillance equipment and methods the UAE government has at their disposal, I don't understand why they can't tell me more. Surely, they know more than they're saying.

My hand rubs my temple as I glare down at my phone, rereading the message. I close the app and switch off my phone, pushing it away from me on the table.

"Here you go. Coffee, chicken on Turkish, and the two boxed-up cakes are in the bag. Was there anything else?" the waitress asks, placing everything on the table.

"No, that's everything. Thanks," I reply, forcing a smile.

She nods. Then, she takes my table number and walks away, clearing some tables as she goes.

I pick at my early lunch and take a sip of the coffee before opening the newspaper. Most of it is reporting on business deals and new construction. Quickly perusing the pages, I note there's nothing about Sarah's abduction or the ongoing investigation. There's nothing at all to indicate any reason for some of the heightened security measures that have subtly been put in place around the schools and some of the malls. Not a damn thing, not that it should really surprise me.

"Mind if I take a seat?" A voice startles me.

I look up in time to see a woman pulling out the chair opposite me and taking a seat.

She looks familiar, but before I can place her, she starts talking again, "This café has the best coffee. Don't you agree?"

"Excuse me, do I know you?" I ask in an uncertain tone.

She smiles before offering her hand across the table. "No, Jennifer. My name is Emilia Curtis. I'm currently on assignment with Human Rights Watch, and I've been hoping to talk with you."

I stare at her hand for a minute, not making any movement to touch it. This was the reporter from the press conference. She looks different today with loose hair, minimal makeup, and casual clothes. I lean away from the table, crossing my arms.

She drops her hand, but her smile doesn't leave her face, not at all ruffled by my defensive posture. "I was hoping you'd call me after the press conference last week. Or after I left a message with your husband's office."

"You called Kevin?" I ask slowly, eyes widening a fraction.

"Well, I tried. I got through to his office once and left a message when he wasn't available. My phone stopped working after that." She reaches into her bag and pulls out a cell phone.

I watch in fascination as she unlocks the screen and holds it up in front of my face.

"See? No signal. It's very strange that the local carriers have blocked my number. You'd think they'd prefer to listen in to what I was saying rather than blocking me completely." She shrugs as though it's not a big deal to openly discuss the Emiratis' habit of monitoring calls.

"What're you talking about?" I feign ignorance, pushing the phone away from me.

"Just another human rights violation. That's what it is," she says, shaking her head.

I really have no idea why she's here or why I should care that her phone's not working. The confusion must show on my face.

"Sorry. Let's start again. My name is Emilia Curtis, and I work for Human Rights Watch. We were tipped off by one of the news outlets in London that the abduction of your daughter might be linked to a human-trafficking ring that's operating here in Dubai …"

My rapid breathing stops her words. She stares at me and waits. I sit motionless as my heart pounds, and my hands shake. Emilia's profile blurs for a second until I blink her back into focus. Her forehead wrinkles as a sad frown crosses her face, and her eyes widen with concern.

"Breathe, Jennifer. Just breathe," she coaxes softly. "That's it."

As my breathing slows, I push my chair back and bend so that my head rests on the edge of the table. Black spots form behind tightly closed eyes as my breathing returns to normal.

"Shit," I mumble. I slowly raise my head and scoot the chair back toward the table. "I'm sorry. It's been a rough couple of weeks."

Emilia smiles gently. "No need to apologize. I can't begin to imagine what you're going through."

"What you're saying about human trafficking isn't true," I say. I inhale through my nose and briefly look away before continuing. "Sarah's missing, and the police are investigating. They'll find her soon."

"Jennifer," Emilia says softly, "we both know that's not true. One of my sources, who previously worked with IOM—the International Organization for Migration—has evidence proving the Dubai Police have made arrests, and one of those people arrested was a member of a known Russian human-trafficking ring. I understand your reluctance to talk to me, given what country we're in and who's investigating your daughter's abduction, but hear me out, please.

"As I said, I work for Human Rights Watch. We specialize in cases like these, and we can help you. What's happening here is a cover-up, and we can help expose the facts and put pressure on the UAE government to respect your and Sarah's human rights and secure justice legally. We're looking to achieve change to the human rights situation here in the Emirates, and we can only do that by reporting facts and demanding the government give us full transparency. It's our mission."

As Emilia talks, my heart races.

I look around the café at the occupants. They all appear to be expats, but it's hard to be sure. Just because there's not a headscarf in sight and everyone's wearing Western-style clothes doesn't mean that they aren't Emirati or Arab. The roof and corners of the room don't appear to have any surveillance cameras, but I'm only looking for what I expect to see. I don't really know what I should be looking for. Countersurveillance is something that belongs in Hollywood movies and not my morning brunch stop.

"I'm sorry. I can't be here right now." I try to stand, but her hand on my arm tightens and keeps me in place.

"Please let me go. I can't talk to you, not now and not here."

"Relax, Jennifer. Just give me five minutes. Five more minutes, and then you'll never have to see or talk to me again."

I nod slowly and scan the room. Even though I can't be seen with her, I want to know what she knows. I want to know if she's privy to information the US Embassy and Dubai Police haven't shared with me. Or information from this other source. IOM is highly respected for their work. Maybe they've seen something that could help us track down Sarah. As long as I listen and don't say anything, I can't be accused of colluding with any reporters.

Emilia removes her hand and sits back in her chair. Her eyes cautiously study me, as though she's waiting for me to flee. I sigh and slump deeper into my chair, picking up my coffee and bringing it to my lips. The lukewarm temperature doesn't diminish the acrid taste, but the joy from sipping it has gone.

"Five minutes," I say, looking at her over my coffee cup.

The small smile on her lips doesn't meet her eyes and disappears quickly when she starts talking, "Okay, so we're aware your daughter was taken from the Mall of the Emirates two weeks ago. The Dubai Police were called to the scene and asked to investigate, and they've apprehended members of a human-trafficking ring operated by people we believe to be associated with the Russian Mafia." She pauses momentarily, her eyes not leaving mine. "I have a source who is an investigative journalist working this region, who confirms the arrests of these people have yet to be formalized. No charges have been lodged against them even though they've supposedly been held for a week and a half now. We believe Sarah's been taken out of the country, but at this stage, we aren't certain of her whereabouts or her final destination. Given the Russian connections, we think she's been taken to one of the Eastern Bloc countries."

I place my cup back onto the table and sigh. "Is that it?"

"You don't seem very surprised. Either you have a great poker face, or I haven't told you anything you don't already know. This tells me you're aware of the cover-up happening at the political level, and … you're being told to keep quiet."

My thumb circles the lip of the coffee mug as I break eye contact with her and look out the window. "If this story you've told me is true, where is Sarah?"

"I don't know. I'm truly sorry, Jennifer."

My hand tightens on the mug at her answer, and my eyes threaten to water. At least she was able to confirm what I'd already known as well as the suspicions that Sarah was out of the country. Emilia feeds into my greatest fear—that Sarah was sold into slavery in one of the countries that makes up the Eastern Bloc. Child prostitution and pornography is rife there, as are young child brides.

"Then, you can't help me …" I whisper almost inaudibly.

A warm hand gently rests on mine, bringing me back to the café. I snatch my hand back and look up into eyes holding both sympathy and determination.

"I can, Jennifer. Human Rights Watch *can* help. We can bring the real story to light and get the government to admit to these travesties of justice operating in their country as well as force them to bring the perpetrators to trial instead of making them disappear. They need to uphold the laws of human decency and stop the human rights violations." Her words are spoken softly and with an assurance I don't feel.

How is any of this going to help find Sarah?

"We need your help. We want you to go on record to tell your story—the *real* story—so we can put a stop to all of this. It's not as though the truth isn't already being speculated in the media in the US and UK anyway."

"I … I can't. Even if everything you said is true, I can't," I whisper, struggling to force each word from my mouth.

What she's suggesting is insane and dangerous for me and my family. Even if it were possible, it wouldn't help us find Sarah. An open investigation would put her life in jeopardy. I need to think of both her and Liam's safety.

"Jennifer, just think—"

I slam my hands down on the table and give her a hard look. "No!" My voice comes out like the steel that's suddenly coursing through my veins. I can't be here, talking to her. It was wrong of me to entertain her. "Listen to me. You've had your five minutes. I have no idea what you're talking about, and I can't help you!" I shout the last words in case anyone in authority is listening.

With a quick glance at my untouched food, I gather up my bagged cake and purse, push back the chair, and stand. Emilia remains seated and watches my preparations to leave. She doesn't push her luck by trying to change my mind or by asking me to stay.

Without a backward look, I walk out the front door, glancing in both directions for the telltale police vehicle, and I head to my car, more than ready to be within the safe walls of my villa.

18

"Liam? Liam, come down for dinner, please," I yell into the vacant stairwell.

A wave of dizziness forces me to grab the banister to steady myself. Maybe I should've made more of an effort to eat something today. A few moments pass before I regain my equilibrium, resigned that I'll have to drag myself upstairs to inform my son that his food is on the table. I think fleetingly that I should text him. It seems like the only way I can communicate with him nowadays.

"Jen! Can you come in here and look at this?"

I jump in surprise at the loud intrusion to my thoughts and turn to see Kevin briefly standing in the doorway to his office. He hasn't been home much at all over the past two weeks, and I've sort of become accustomed to not expecting him or having him around. The hands on my watch face are surely playing tricks with me. It's a rarity for Kevin to be home from the office so early during the week.

"Coming." With a final glance at the stairs, I head along the hallway to Kevin's office.

Liam can wait a few more minutes.

"Hey, honey. I didn't know you were home. We were just about to have dinner. I can fix you …" My words trail off as I look at what's caught Kevin's attention.

He stands behind his desk, hands clenched. The BBC news is playing on the television mounted on the far wall. My body shakes as I see who is on the panel being interviewed and read the breaking news headline under her name.

"… it's a problem for the Middle East and Northern Africa as a whole. We've seen it in Sudan with their border control colluding with human traffickers and the Sudanese authorities and taking bribes to keep it quiet rather than stepping up to investigate them. On one occasion, a non-governmental organization, or an NGO, operating along the border area tried to provide assistance to a group of potential trafficking victims and relocate them into refugee camps or return them home. What resulted in this instance was criminal prosecution of the trafficking victims."

The HRW person, Emilia Curtis, is sitting on a panel with two other people talking to *BBC News at Six* presenter Ben Thompson. Hair pulled back in a chignon with perfectly applied makeup, she looks every ounce the professional.

I watch in morbid fascination as the camera pans to put Ben in full frame as he speaks. "So, you have people seeking safety and a better way of life and others being sold into slavery. I would expect to hear about people smuggling, human trafficking, and other criminal activities that violate human rights in war-torn countries where the regime's policing is not fully established or has the potential to be corrupted. But to hear about human trafficking in countries deemed to be stable, prosperous, and an accepted member of the international community …"

"Shit … shit … shit …"

My eyes are drawn to Kevin as he shakes his head while muttering under his breath. His attention is glued to the screen.

"What does the recent abduction of Sarah Johnson in Dubai say about this, and what we can believe to be happening in other affluent cities of the Middle East?"

My ears perk up at the use of Sarah's name, and I return my attention to the television.

"Exactly, Ben. I think you've hit on a key word there—*affluent*. Cities in the region—cities like Cairo, Amman, Beirut, Kuwait City, Dubai—all have an affluent ruling body or are rich in resources or have high tourism turnover. We often overlook these countries when we think of criminal elements conducting human trafficking, but they're the perfect environments for it to occur. All these countries import their working class from the developing world, mainly South Asian countries. Human rights violations occur and are being covered up. There is also a long-standing problem of trafficking in women, including Western women, for prostitution and forced marriage.

"We believe an organized ring involved in such activity targeted Sarah Johnson for abduction, and as she is a US citizen, it's brought the dark underbelly of the city to light. But, because it's a regional business hub and fast becoming a leading tourist destination for Europe and the world, the authorities are trying to cover it up.

"HRW has learned from certain sources that they've detained people with links to the Russian Mafia and a human-trafficking ring. The organization takes women and children from the Middle East, Northern Africa, and South Asia and sells them into slavery and prostitution in Eastern Bloc countries. Our sources have confirmed that these people have been detained and questioned, but they've yet to be arrested or scheduled for trial."

The room suddenly spins, and I plant a hand against the wall to gain equilibrium. The wine I drank earlier threatens to find its way out as my stomach churns. With effort, I swallow it back and watch the Q & A between the panel and Ben play out.

The newsreader starts. "Last week, we saw the parents of the missing girl make an emotional plea to the public for information on her whereabouts. Interpol has said they're looking into it. The US Embassy in Dubai has said they're working closely with the UAE government in finding her. They're saying she's a missing person. Why is that?"

"It's simple, Ben. They can't say anything else. The country Sarah Johnson disappeared from doesn't allow freedom of speech. It persecutes those who speak out against them. I think it's a case of doing and saying what you are told. I believe that doing so is a disservice to this young girl and won't help to find her. I told the mother, Mrs. Johnson, this last week when I spoke with her."

My hand covers my mouth as I gasp in shock. A cold sweat has broken on my brow. My eyes leave the screen and focus on Kevin as the on-screen dialogue continues.

"What did she say?"

"She didn't say much. She appeared scared for her safety. But she did confirm that there was more going on than had been said."

"Have there been any updates to the investigation into Sarah Johnson's abduction?"

"No. Our sources indicate she's been spirited out of the country. My main concern, and the concern of my organization, is the lack of transparency by the UAE government and our need for them to respect the rights of their victims and the criminals they have detained ..."

Kevin mutes the audio and throws the remote across the room, but he keeps staring at the screen, his frame vibrating. "Jen ... when did you talk to this ... person? Why did you talk to her?" he demands, lips pursed and breathing deeply.

"I-I didn't talk to her. She approached me a few days ago in a café, but I told her to go away." I shake my head as though the action will erase the memory of the BBC interview from my mind. If only it were that easy.

Kevin turns toward me, eyes lit with fury. "You must have said something. She said you did."

I walk to the couch and drop into it. My body slumps back in defeat. I close my eyes. When I speak, my words come out hoarse. "She's lying. She sat at my table. She started saying all this stuff about Human Rights Watch and IOM and suggested the Dubai Police were perpetrating a cover-up." I look directly at Kevin. "I told her she was wrong and said I didn't know what she was talking about."

"Goddamn it, Jen. How could you put yourself in that position? Fuck!"

I flinch at his harsh words.

He kicks the office chair back toward the wall. It rolls across the tiled floor and crashes into the wall before ricocheting back. He pushes it out of the way and paces between the bookshelves and his desk.

With a guttural growl, Kevin stops and turns to face me. His face is twisted in an ugly grimace. He places his hands behind his head and looks up to the ceiling, as though the answers to all of life's problems could be found, written there. "Fuck!"

"I didn't do anything wrong." My words are gentle as I try not to add fuel to the already blazing inferno. Judging by the dark look he shoots my way, it doesn't work.

"I don't think you realize the severity of your actions. You royally screwed things up for us. Fuck!"

With effort, I stand and walk slowly toward him with the intention of providing support. "Kev—"

"No. Don't fucking touch me. I can't bear the thought of you at the moment."

The screen on the cell phone sitting on the desk lights up, indicating incoming messages. He picks it up and unlocks the screen to scroll through them, cursing under his breath before violently shoving it into his back pocket.

"You know what? I can't be here now. I can't be here with you. I need to go and get a drink. Might as well have a few before I'm called into the office to answer questions about your fuckup," he says, tone ice-cold.

He shuffles some paperwork into a pile on his desk and slides them into his briefcase.

Kevin brushes past me and continues out the front door. Frustration turns to anger as I watch him through the window as he starts his car and drives away. My gaze drifts to the broken remote and then up to the muted television screen. This is not my fault. If he'd taken the time to really listen to my words and explanation, maybe he'd have seen that.

The program flicks over to the weather, and I'm not surprised to see tomorrow's going to be hot and humid.

When is it not?

19

I sigh as the *muezzin*'s call to morning prayer from the neighborhood mosque summons the faithful to the daily ritual of submission to their God, Allah. Normally, I'd still be asleep, conditioned to slumber through the melodic sound, but my churning thoughts kept me restless for most of the night. Bedsheets tangled around my body tighten their hold as I roll over to look at the empty space beside me.

Kevin didn't come back last night. Well, I don't think he did. He might be in the guest room downstairs, but I doubt it. It's frustrating, just as much as it is annoying. The constant anger he's been projecting can't be good for him. It's not pleasant for me, and it's definitely not for Liam. If only he'd take the time to sit and listen and let us work through these problems together instead of keeping all his feelings bottled inside. These compressed feelings erupt in a fit of rage, and it's not healthy. Melanie's right; we need someone to help us work through this. Sooner rather than later.

The buzzing of my alarm forces me to extricate myself from the bed to start the day. I groan, thinking about all of the people who are going to want to talk to me today. The BBC story stirred everyone's emotions, leaving me apprehensive about going outside the villa's walls. I have to though. Liam's leaving on a school trip today, and I need to drop him off. I can always lock myself in the villa after he leaves and barricade myself from reality. The problem is, real life will still be waiting, and the issues I don't want to deal with will find their way to me regardless. Kevin, fallout from the BBC story, the police investigation … and Sarah.

I close my eyes and sigh. If life were a fairy tale, I'd patiently endure the conflict and turmoil if I knew my happily ever after was to come. Give it to me now. I'm ready for it. But it's not, and I can't.

I have to get up and deal with the consequences. Reluctantly, I try to find a silver lining, a sliver of hope. Who knows? Maybe the story will have some positive outcomes.

"If wishes were horses …" I whisper the start of the old proverb and stand to stretch out my tired limbs, not quite ready to start the day.

Beggars would ride …

———

The doorbell chime echoes loudly through the villa. I put my coffee cup down. It's too early for visitors, which means the aftermath from last night's news is about to begin.

"I'll get that, madam," Anika says, walking past the kitchen doorway, mop in hand.

I smile to myself, picturing the Ethiopian lady hitting any unwelcome guests with it. If it's Monica or Jacquie, I'm sure Anika will take much joy in hitting them as well.

"Is Dad coming to see me off?" Liam asks hopefully.

I fight very hard for my smile not to transform into a grimace as I remember how Kevin and I left things last night. Or the manner of his leaving.

"Yes, I'm going to call him soon to make sure of it."

"Madam? Madam, it is the police officer, wanting you at the front door," Anika says, entering the kitchen through the door from the dining room.

"Liam, we'll be heading off to school shortly. Can you go and grab your bag? I'll wait for you out front."

I stand and move out of the way as Anika starts clearing the breakfast dishes. Steam rises from the sink as she fills it with hot water. I have no idea why she prefers to wash everything by hand; we do own a dishwasher. I suppose dish hands and the effect they have on your manicure isn't a concern for her. As Anika sinks her hands into the soapy water and starts humming a tune, I reluctantly leave the kitchen to find out who exactly is gracing us with their presence this morning.

"Mrs. Johnson, is your husband home?" Lieutenant Ahmed's words bring me to a halt on my way to the door.

Anika must have let him in and asked him to wait in Kevin's office. He stands as I enter.

"Good morning, Lieutenant. No, I'm sorry. Kevin's already at the office." I slightly turn away from him at the lie. "Do you have news on Sarah?"

Lieutenant Ahmed uncomfortably looks away, running his hands down the dark blue of his tailored uniform pants in an effort to reduce the wrinkles. "No, Mrs. Johnson. I have nothing new to share with you regarding the investigation of your missing daughter. My visit here this morning is for reasons not very pleasant. We saw the news story on the BBC last night and are deeply offended by what the Human Rights Watch and reporters are saying about Dubai and the UAE. You were aware that talking to the press and divulging information about the open investigation would affect the integrity of our investigation," he says accusingly. "The government guidelines are very clear on—"

"Lieutenant Ahmed," I cut in before he can finish.

His posture stiffens, and his eyes harden at the interruption.

"I'm sorry to interrupt, but we didn't talk to the media. I didn't talk to that reporter. She approached me in a café and said a bunch of stuff, and I left."

"The transcripts we have of the BBC interview have the HRW spokesperson, Ms. Emilia Curtis, quoting you and—"

"I know what she said, Lieutenant," I say forcefully, stopping him again mid-sentence. "Believe me, I know. Kevin and I saw it on the television last night and are both outraged at what was said. It's a lie. I never said anything to her. Kevin and I are both very upset about it. About everything."

I shake my head, take a deep breath, and look directly into the lieutenant's cold eyes before continuing quietly. "You have to understand. We would never do anything to jeopardize your investigation or put at risk your efforts to find our daughter."

My plea must sink in because his demeanor relaxes slightly. It doesn't, however, stop the interrogation.

"You were seen talking to her at the Lime Tree Café, Mrs. Johnson."

"Yes, I'm sure I was. I was there, picking up cake and getting some lunch, when she approached me. *She* sat down at *my* table and started talking to *me*. I asked her to leave, but she was rather persistent. Whoever told you I was there with her should have also told you that I got up and left—without my lunch. I'm sure, if there's some sort of security footage of the café, it would also confirm the truth of what happened. *She* approached *me*, and like the first time she reached out, I ignored her." It takes effort to keep my voice steady.

I'm hedging my bets on any video surveillance in the café not having audio, just like the one I saw in the Mall of the Emirates. I'm guilty by default. I might not have discussed or confirmed anything with Emilia, but I didn't exactly deny anything she'd said either. The lieutenant doesn't need to know that. Any admission of guilt on my behalf would probably have me arrested and see the investigation into Sarah's abduction stopped and somehow buried.

"You have seen this Human Rights Watch person before?" the lieutenant asks, closely watching me.

I dip my head in a curt nod before responding, "Yes. She was at the press interview held at the consulate the week before last. I didn't talk to her that time either. She slipped me a note, asking to meet, but I ignored it. This is why she approached me at the café." I shrug and turn away.

There's not much I can do to convince him. He'll either believe me or not.

"How do I know you did not contact her to organize the meeting at the café?"

His eyes narrow, trying to intimidate me and almost succeeding.

A chuckle escapes as I shake my head. I turn back to face him, the smile on my face not meeting my eyes. "I didn't contact her. I'm sure my phone records will verify this. And hers, too. I'm certain you can access them if you choose to do so."

Lieutenant Ahmed intently watches me, the silence stretching out uncomfortably. "Okay then. There is an increase in reporters out on the street. We will be keeping a permanent police presence near your family to make sure there are no more misunderstandings."

His dress shoes click on the bare tiles as he marches past me and out of the office. I follow him to the front door, hoping to get an indication as to the current status of their investigation into Sarah's abduction.

"You'll let us know if you find out anything new regarding Sarah?"

His shoes glide easily on the sheen of sand covering the front porch as he turns. "Mrs. Johnson, let us hope this latest development in the media does not affect our investigation. I am hoping for both you and your daughter's sake. *Ma'salaama.*"

With those final words and his veiled threat, the lieutenant turns and leaves. I watch him slide into the back seat of his car, and the driver pulls away from the curb.

The BBC story struck a chord with me. The words they were using and the discussion between the Human Rights Watch reporter and the BBC correspondent are playing over and over in my mind.

What if they're correct and there is some sort of a cover-up happening? What if all we've been doing for the past two and a half weeks is wasting time and energy while being misled by the UAE government? There has to be a better way to find Sarah. *But why would the US government advise us to go along with the Dubai Police?* It's as though they washed their hands of us once it was determined Sarah hadn't been kidnapped. I'm sure they didn't, but it feels that way.

"Mom, was that Lieutenant Ahmed? What did he want? Have they found Sarah?" Liam says from behind, startling me.

Hands over my chest, I take a deep breath. He sounded hesitantly hopeful, and my heart aches for him.

"Yes, it was. And, no, they haven't found her yet, honey." My words are said gently as I wrap my arm around his shoulders in reassurance. I smile sadly down at him and realize our shoulders are almost at the same level. He's growing more into a man every day. "Let me get my keys and bag and get you to school. You must be excited for your trip, right?"

I leave Liam standing on the front porch and prepare for the school run. His silhouette in the morning light doesn't reflect that of a twelve-year-old child. His long, lanky limbs give away his youth, but his pensive demeanor offers an air of maturity. Liam stands contemplative, backpack over one shoulder, as he waits.

"Let's go." I nudge his shoulder, and we head for the car.

It's with relief that I note the absence of any overt reporters as we leave our street. That might or might not have something to do with the police car stationed at the corner. I offer a small wave to the police officers as we drive past.

We turn onto Sheikh Zayed Road when Liam airs his thoughts, words laced with a touch of fear. "Why was the police lieutenant at the house, Mom? What's going on?"

"One of the news channels interviewed some people from Human Rights Watch, and they discussed Sarah's disappearance. The story aired last night on TV, and it's now also trending online." With hands that grip the steering wheel so tightly that my knuckles whiten, I stop to ponder how best to continue. "Basically, they've come up with some theories as to where Sarah could be and why she was taken. It wasn't very complimentary to the UAE or the Dubai Police. Lieutenant Ahmed wanted to remind us not to talk to anyone about the investigation, especially not any reporters. So, if anyone asks you what's going on, you'll just have to tell them that you can't talk about it. Okay?"

Liam nods in understanding. As we take the exit ramp and turn onto the street that leads to the side gate of the school, he whispers, "I hope they find her soon."

I do, too.

A mother's love knows no bounds. It's untainted and endless.

My heart hurts as I look at the concern and compassion on Liam's face. My heart breaks as I remember the reason it's there. I wish I could take away his pain. I wish he didn't have to deal with this situation and the unanswered questions about his sister. There's so much I wish for.

20

The bus taking Liam's class on their day trip is parked near the side gate to the school. I pull into a parking spot not too far away. The kids are taking the two-hour drive to the Emirati capital to visit the new Louvre Abu Dhabi as part of their ancient civilizations studies. The museum not only houses art, but it is also a work of art in itself.

Kevin and I attended the grand opening. I will never forget the awe I felt as sunlight filtered through the web-patterned dome roof, providing an ethereal feeling. The architecture and design of it are amazing.

In light of everything, I was a bit hesitant about allowing Liam on the trip. Knowing he was more than just a phone call and a quick fifteen-minute drive away made me feel uneasy, but his counselor and teachers convinced me that it would be okay. They also promised that, if any issues arose, they'd be able to get him home early.

"Okay, Liam, let's get you onto the bus," I say, releasing my seat belt and opening the car door.

We go around to the back of the car, and Liam grabs his backpack and throws it over his shoulder. I look toward the bus, only now noticing the police car parked off to the side. A group of ten people or so are loitering at the rear of the bus. They don't appear to be parents dropping their kids off. One has a camera and is standing next to a guy with a microphone. As though a signal flare has been lit, they burst into life and start toward us as we make our way to the bus.

"Shit," I mumble under my breath.

I recognize a few of them as parents from the school. I'm hoping it's all just a coincidence and they're having an impromptu meeting and not waiting around for me. Their eyes are focused on our progression toward the bus, and most hold grim expressions.

"Why are those people looking at us like that? Who are they?" Liam asks nervously, pulling his shoulders back as he moves closer to me.

My young protector.

"A reporter and a photographer? And some parents, I think?"

I'm not sure, but it looks like they've been waiting to talk to me. I can't fault them for that. I suppose if I were a parent and had seen the news, I would want answers as well. And who better to provide those answers? If they're waiting for me, that's one thing. Being parents themselves, they should have the decency to realize that I have Liam with me, and he shouldn't be exposed to the sort of questions I'm guessing they want to throw at me. Hesitantly, I look at our car, wondering if there's time to escape. Unfortunately, this isn't an option.

With a deep breath, I pull my shoulders back and resign myself to deal with this head-on. "Liam, pull your cap down lower so they can't photograph your face."

The group, followed closely by two police officers, converges on us before we can make it to the bus. I recognize one of the ladies as the mother of one of Sarah's classmates.

"Jennifer! Jen, can we have a word?" she calls out.

"Mrs. Johnson, do you have anything to say about the claims that your daughter was taken and sold off into slavery?" the reporter asks as a camera flashes in my eyes. "What about the incompetence with the investigation? Do you have anything to say about that?"

I put my arm around Liam and try to shield him as the parents stop and look at each other, listening to the reporter's questions.

"Or that the local authorities know who took your daughter and allowed her to leave the country?"

"Please … I have my son here. Can I please drop him off?" I ask. My forced confidence is undercut by the quiver in my voice. Hands clammy and trembling, they tighten on Liam's shoulders as I direct him through the crowd toward the bus.

The press's reaction from last night's BBC interview has unmistakably taken an aggressive turn. It might be only one reporter, but he's definitely not shying away from asking any hard questions.

"Jennifer! Jennifer, over here." Deborah Ferguson, ASD's middle school principal, gestures for us to approach her.

I watch in horror as the police move through the small crowd in an attempt to grab the reporter. The reporter thwarts their efforts and ducks in front of a cameraman. A smaller crowd of parents, housemaids, drivers, and students has stopped on the sidewalk to watch in fascination, some with their cell phones out, filming the disturbance. Cars on the road are at a standstill as the commotion brings more unwanted attention.

"Mrs. Johnson, is it true that you've been silenced? Why did you refuse to pay the ransom?"

A loud burst from a police siren startles both Liam and me. Flashing lights pull my attention to a police car that's driven up on the footpath behind us, announcing the arrival of reinforcements. The cameraman observes their arrival and tries subtly to pack away his equipment while slowly shuffling in the opposite direction. Onlookers only pay a cursory glance at the intrusion, focusing their attention on the lone reporter creating the spectacle by shouting questions at me.

"What's the connection to the Russian Mafia? Are they responsible for all the missing children in the region? Are the Russians behind a child porn ring?"

The police, who snuck up behind him, pull the reporter to the side. He twists away and pushes the officer, toppling the mom from Sarah's class onto the paved sidewalk. The action does nothing to deter the police officer as he regains his balance and grabs the reporter, placing him in a stress hold, arm wrenched behind him, and forcing him toward the police car. This action has the parents scrambling to move out of the way.

"*Yalla!*" A deep voice from behind makes me flinch and draws my attention away from the scene. Lieutenant Ahmed stands impatiently, his beret crooked across his forehead, emphasizing the thick eyebrows that are pinched together. "Mrs. Johnson, is your son meant to be going on the bus today?"

I incline my head slightly, and he shouts orders to a policeman standing on the other side of the crowd to escort Liam and me to the bus. "Muhammad, *raafiqhum lil hafila. Halla!*"

I offer Muhammad a small smile as he walks us through the gathered crowd and to the waiting principal.

"Liam, we're so glad you could make it. How about you say goodbye to your mom and wait on the bus with the other students?" she says cheerfully.

Liam nods, envelops me in a hug, and whispers, "You know, I could stay home and keep you company if you want. I don't need to go today. I'm sure they'd give me a pass if I asked for one."

"Nice try, kid. No. You'll have fun and hopefully learn something new."

I totally agree with him. I was hesitant to allow him to go with everything going on. I only agreed after talking to Liam's grief counselor as well as the school counselor and his teachers. They've been telling me all along that Liam needs a normal routine and to be around kids his own age. So, I've been trying to do that for him.

"What if …" He trails off as he watches something going on in the crowd behind me. It's probably the police telling everyone to move along.

"I'll call you if we hear anything. You can call me as well if you need to," I say, holding back the tears.

I know my fears of losing another child are unfounded and ridiculous, but they exist nonetheless. He's going to be on some bus, traveling two hours away from me, not spending a few hours in school behind tall concrete walls. It feels different.

"Okay, Liam, off you go. You can check in with your mom later," Mrs. Ferguson says.

I wave as he climbs aboard, the dark-tinted door closing behind him.

"I'm sorry about your reception this morning," Mrs. Ferguson says quietly to me. Her voice remains low as she continues to scan the area, her features grim. "We called the police to have the reporters escorted away, but they only arrived a few minutes before you did. We did ask the reporter and his photographer not to take any images of the children or school property, and they seemed pretty polite … until you arrived."

"I'm so sorry."

She places a hand on my shoulder. "Hush now. There's no need to apologize. Judging by what I just saw, it's probably a good thing Liam will be away from the school today. We can get this under control and sorted before tomorrow. The last thing we need is for him to be approached by any parents on school grounds. Or hear other kids repeating whatever their parents are saying at home. No, we'll set something up today, so he won't have to deal with it tomorrow. Today, he'll have the anonymity at the museum as part of the school crowd as well."

The principal walks away to talk to one of the other teachers and compare notes on their clipboards. She has a valid point. I didn't even consider Liam being approached by overzealous parents within the school grounds. Reassured he'll be in capable hands, I turn to find Lieutenant Ahmed facing me.

"Mrs. Johnson, this is the sort of thing we want to avoid and is also why we don't talk to the press," he scolds. He continues before I can point out that, other than the press conference sponsored by the US Embassy, I haven't spoken to any reporters. "Go home. Your presence is causing problems."

There's a tremor in my voice as I respond. "Yes, Lieutenant." I lick my lips and take a last look at the bus, seeing the last of the teachers board.

Other parents and caregivers are waving as it slowly pulls away from the curb. I raise my hand and say a silent farewell to Liam before heading back to my car. To my left, two police officers have the reporter in handcuffs beside the patrol car. Another officer has dispersed the crowd of onlookers on the sidewalk by his mere presence.

As I turn the ignition, I glance to my rearview mirror in time to see the reporter being forced into a patrol car.

I pull out of the lot and head toward home. Through the Bluetooth phone connection, I call Kevin. Unsurprisingly, he doesn't answer. With hands still shaking from the unexpected ambush, I wait for his recorded greeting to finish before leaving a message.

"Kevin, I need you to call me back. Lieutenant Ahmed came to the villa this morning, asking questions about whether we spoke to the Human Rights Watch person, and he wasn't too happy. Anyway, I just dropped Liam off at school. There were some concerned parents and a reporter waiting, and it got messy. You were meant to be there." I pause momentarily and take a deep breath to calm my nerves. I continue in a whisper. "You need to come home, Kevin. We need to sit down and talk through everything to make sure we're on the same page. There can't be any more misunderstandings or fuckups. Call me back, please. Or just come home. Tonight, we need to talk."

The drive home occurs on autopilot in the silence of my car. Before I realize where I am or what I am doing, I've already parked. A chime indicating a received SMS alerts me to my cell phone. The locked screen illuminates the text of the message.

I'll be home after work. Talk then.

21

It doesn't take long for me to realize the BBC story made the rounds and has everybody talking. I took a few calls before switching off my phone. Even though I know everyone's concerned and wondering if Sarah's abduction impacts them and their safety, it angers me that they think it's their right to get answers. Especially when I don't have them. Their tactless questions pierce my heart and eat away at my soul. It should've upset me when the reporter who accosted me outside the school asked openly if it was true about the government covering up a child pornography ring. But the question didn't upset me. Being ambushed and exposing Liam to the scene did. The reporter's probably sitting in a dank cell now, pondering his life decisions as he faces charges and deportation.

The police intervention at the school sobered anyone trying to approach me pretty quick. Even the reporters I'd seen out and about and who'd been keeping their distance the past few weeks have completely disappeared. The threat of a jail cell for breaking local laws sent the message loud and clear. In a way, I'm glad. Nobody wants stalking paparazzi trying to get the perfect shot even if it's only of my abysmal existence. It's more harassing than helpful. Photos of me wearing sweats to the grocery store or sitting behind the wheel of my car with dark glasses on aren't going to help us find Sarah.

The villa offers sanctuary from the madness, which is a good thing. Kevin promised to be home tonight, and we're going to finally talk and clear the air. It's way past due. I just hope his anger has abated and he's willing to listen to my side of the story. As in I didn't do or say anything.

This seems to be my mantra today. I said it to Lieutenant Ahmed when he visited earlier this morning. George from the embassy arrived on my doorstep around lunchtime, asking similar questions, annoyed with the way the media was playing it out and with me having my phone switched off. I told him the same thing I'd told Lieutenant Ahmed. When some concerned school parents knocked, I ordered Anika to tell them I wasn't home or that I was sleeping. I feel completely useless—and trapped.

A dark cloud hovers over me, and I'm fearful of my premonition that it's only going to get worse. With these macabre thoughts in mind, I find myself in Sarah's room, lying on her bed. I bring her pillow to my face, and tears threaten to fall when I realize it doesn't smell of her. Instead of her girlish, flowery scent, I'm met with lavender fabric softener. Anika has changed the linen, washed her clothes, and turned her room into an empty, sterile place. I refuse to believe this is a sign for what is to come.

———

Thankfully, Liam's field trip to the Louvre Abu Dhabi was uneventful.

Before collecting Liam, I met with Deborah to discuss the plan she'd devised to protect him from overly curious and aggressive parents within school grounds. An email advisory will be sent out this evening to the parents and guardians of all ASD students as well as the teachers, outlining the new protocols.

Liam and I spoke about what to expect during the car ride home.

I think about this and our discussion while walking the pizza upstairs for him to eat in front of his computer and television. Bad parenting, I know, but he'll more than likely be in the zone until he puts himself to bed, and I definitely don't want him coming downstairs, looking for snacks and accidentally overhearing Kevin and me.

Right now, I'm bracing myself for my talk with Kevin. A whole lot needs to be said. I also need answers. I walk slowly down the stairs, internally debating whether I should prepare myself with some liquid courage. Before I can decide, I hear movement in the sitting room by the pool.

Kevin.

He's home.

Kevin's pouring himself a whiskey as I walk into the room. He regards me, bringing the tumbler filled with amber liquid to his lips. At least he's looking at me tonight. With the world crumbling around us, he should be here for us. Making sure everything is okay, that we are okay. Things have remained tense between us since Sarah's abduction, but I thought, after our emotional plea to the public the other week with the media, we'd hit the turning point. I assumed we had finally connected in our grief and were in sync, ready to move past all the anger. I was really hoping he was ready to join me in counseling. But that was before the BBC reporting.

I need my husband back. I'm sick of being alone.

"Do you want a drink?" he asks in an even tone, not breaking eye contact with me.

I try to smile. "Yes, please." My nerves are fried, and a drink might help settle them. I take the glass, hand shaking slightly.

"So, what was with the voicemail you left this morning? And why am I receiving emails from Deborah Ferguson about special protocols put in place for Liam at the school?" He takes a seat and crosses one leg over the other, leaning back into the chair as though he were conducting a business meeting at the office. He sits patiently and waits for my response.

With the look he's giving me, you'd think I was one of his young employees trying to justify why I shouldn't be fired. This irritates me, but I fight to maintain my calm.

"After what aired last night on the BBC, a group of parents as well as a reporter were waiting to question me."

His eyebrows rise with my words.

I place the tumbler on the coffee table and take a seat opposite him. I sit back, mirroring his pose. With a sigh, I continue. "My message was to let you know that we were ambushed at the bus pickup area and that the police had to disperse the crowd. They arrested the reporter. This was after he raised almost every conspiracy possible as a question in front of everybody."

I break eye contact and pick up the tumbler to bring it to my lips. He remains shrouded in his silence.

"You were supposed to be there to see Liam off this morning," I whisper. "You promised to be here when he left for school."

"When did I promise that?" he asks in a clipped tone, sitting forward in his chair.

"The other night, before dinner."

Before we saw the news yesterday, before he left … again.

He sits back, shaking his head. "I don't remember that. And what's so important that I have to see him off to school? He's not a toddler anymore."

A dry laugh escapes before I can control it as I stare at him in astonishment. "Why? Because he's your son, and he hardly sees you at the best of times. And right now, he's distraught over his sister, and he's trying desperately to cover up his feelings. He needs to know that you care, that you're there for him. For us," I finish, my voice shaking, ending in a whisper.

With a nervous gulp, I stand and start pacing, agitated. I can't believe he is acting like this. Frustrated, I sit and bring the whisky to my mouth again. The fiery liquid works its magic as its numbing attributes start to take effect.

"Of course I'm here. Of course I care. You're right; I am his father," he says, giving me a hard stare.

At a loss for words, I fidget with the glass. There's a wall between us, disrupting the lines of communication. Messages are being sent, but none are getting through accurately or in a timely manner.

He sighs, placing his empty tumbler on the table. "Why was he going on a field trip anyway? I thought we'd agreed, and the embassy agreed, that he'd only be going between the house and the school until we worked out the risk to the family. I never signed off on this field trip."

"You didn't have to. I did. If you'd spent more time at home and engaged with us, you would've known about the trip. We discussed it over the past few days, and you would've known that I ran it by George at the embassy."

"Jen—" he starts tersely.

I sit up straight and prepare for a fight. It's obvious that's exactly what he wants.

"What, Kevin? What? You want to play the father card today?"

There goes any calm we had. Any semblance of decent rapport I hoped to build has quickly disintegrated. It makes me sad that he's been so closed off that he's missing out on the things Liam and I have been doing and dealing with. And it makes me infuriated that he thinks he can step back in and demand to be ruler of the world.

We've hardly seen him. He was around in the beginning, in the initial forty-eight hours when we thought Sarah's kidnappers would call with a ransom demand. But since we learned of the trafficking ring, he's become closed off and unreachable.

In all seriousness, regarding this school trip, I did have my initial concerns. I tried to call Kevin and ask his opinion, but he was always unreachable.

His phone rings out or goes straight to voicemail. His secretary refuses to put me through because he is always in meetings or busy or out of the office and promises to pass my messages on. He can be angry all he wants, but he has no one but himself to blame for it. I've given him every opportunity to take an interest in our semblance of living. It's bad enough that we have no control over the investigation and no way of keeping in the loop of what's going on with it. We've been begging for scraps and hoping the authorities will take pity and give us some information.

But Kevin's attitude and demeanor? It's as though he's switched off from the family. I know he's trying to deal with strong emotions, but this isn't the time to give up. With the possibility of hiring a private security company to help chase leads, Interpol putting Sarah on a watch list, and the Dubai Police continuing with their investigation, all is not lost.

"I have to work. If I don't work, then we can't stay here," he snaps, voice rising in volume and intensity. His eyes flash with outrage, and they seem to accuse me of being at fault.

"What are you doing to make this right? What the hell are you doing?" Heartbeat pounding, my vision blurs, and I clench my teeth to stop an additional outburst. I'm not sure where his ire is coming from, but mine is because I have had enough. With hands clenched tight, I jump up and walk to the back door, barely controlling my need to punch something. "Work? How are you able to work? Our daughter is gone. You're not around. What the hell is going on with you?"

"I'm doing everything possible. You need to lay off. My hands are tied to a degree. We're walking a fine line at the moment." He stands and walks over to the armoire to pour himself another whisky.

"How?"

He spins toward me and takes a long sip from his glass, staring at me with cold eyes. "The PR department at work has gotten involved. They don't want this thing dragged out in the media any longer. Apparently, the Emirati government is putting pressure on the company to get this story under wraps, or they'll look at remedial action."

Kevin's too calm, too considered.

Has he forgotten about his daughter? He sounds more worried about his job than Sarah.

"Remedial action? Like what?" I ask incredulously, wondering where he's going with this.

"They've started to review the business license to operate within the UAE and have called HR for their files so they can review all of the current visas on issue—mine included." He looks down at his shaking hands, voice monotone.

"What does that mean for us?" I whisper.

George warned me to be careful when dealing with the media. He said the UAE government would deal with any slight, whether perceived or real. Our continued stay in the country is completely at their discretion.

"It means that *we* need to stop talking to the media. *We* need to rely on the local authorities to resolve this situation without the media circus."

Media circus? He might as well have slapped me.

"We've done everything right! I've done everything right!"

I've done everything I've been told even though it went against everything I wanted to do or say. The only faux pas was the conversation with Emilia Curtis from the Human Rights Watch ... but that was all one-sided. Everything she went on to say and report was just conjecture; it didn't come from anything I said.

I glare at Kevin. "Do you hear yourself? Rely on the local authorities to resolve *this situation*. *This situation* is your ten-year-old daughter being kidnapped! Or have you forgotten?" I slam my fists into the arm of the chair in frustration.

I'm so glad Liam's in his room with his headphones on. I'd hate for him to witness another shouting match.

"No, I've not forgotten! You think I don't know what's at stake? You think I don't wonder how the fuck this is all going to play out? You think I don't think about how this all happened in the first place?" he vehemently spits out.

The look of disgust on his face stops me cold.

I freeze. "What do you mean by that?"

"Nothing. I don't mean anything by it." He shakes his head, but the hard glint in his eyes as he says the words tell me he did mean something by it.

"No, obviously you do, or you wouldn't have said it. What do you mean about how this happened? How do you think it happened? Some stranger coerced our daughter to leave the shop with her, and no one did anything to stop them."

"Yes … but how did it get to that point? How could she be in a position to be *coerced*? How—"

"What the fuck are you trying to say?" I cut him off as my stillness remains. My words are spoken softly, succinctly, and laced with ice-cold venom. "Are you blaming me? Are you saying I'm at fault here? Just spit it out, Kevin. Say what you mean!" Rapid blinking brings my gaze back into focus as I stare at him in disbelief.

Kevin closes his eyes and inhales deeply. Shoulders hunched, he rocks back onto his heels. Opening his eyes, he looks directly at me with a visibly defeated look. "Yes, I do wonder what you were doing and how you could let Sarah wander around, unsupervised."

"And there it is. Fuck." I collapse forward into the chair with my elbows on my thighs, hands covering my face, gently rocking back and forward. If only the tears could come. What's needed now are hot, angry tears, but they won't come.

The events of the past few days have stolen all my tears, the same way those assholes stole my daughter.

22

———

"He's currently in a meeting, Mrs. Johnson. I'll let him know you're here, but it might be a while before he can see you."

The consul general's assistant has led me into an informal meeting room to wait. Like the last time when I was here with Kevin, there's coffee and water on the table in the corner. I nod and fix a fake smile to my face, trying to appear thankful.

"Thank you." I say the words just in case she can't garner it from my expression. She probably can't.

Her small smile in return lets me know she's sympathetic. That's all that matters.

After the door closes and I'm left to my own devices, I find I can't sit. My nerves are on edge. Walking the length of the room, I turn and walk back. Fifteen steps from one side to the other. As I pace the room, thinking about my current situation, I can't help but see how easily I gave over my control. To the embassy staff, the police ... to Kevin.

I've had enough. I'm sick of standing on the sideline. Sarah's been missing for close to three weeks now, and I've been nothing but a good wife, mother, obedient citizen. I've tried to do what they wanted and continue living each day with the status quo. Live as though one of my reasons for breathing wasn't ripped from my heart, stolen from my life. Sit back and wait for the men to work through the problems and update me when they remember or when they can be bothered. I've never felt more like a second-class citizen than in this exact moment. And maybe all the moments in the past three weeks have been leading to this one. No, scratch that. Realistically looking at this, it's been happening since the moment I gave up most of my rights by agreeing to live in this forsaken country.

Today, I'm outraged. Today, I want to take my life back, starting with asserting myself in the search for my daughter. I didn't realize until last night, when Kevin effectively admitted that he blamed me entirely for Sarah's abduction, that I harbored guilt deep down. Even though I know her abduction isn't my fault, I still carry the blame in my soul. What mother wouldn't? What mother wouldn't give her all to get her child back? What mother wouldn't fight?

I sit, leaning over the table, eyes closed with my head in my hands. What sort of mother indeed. I was the mother who tried to keep it all together, to be strong for my son. For my family. But playing by the rules and suppressing my instincts and emotions because they aren't culturally acceptable or could have me arrested hasn't brought Sarah back and hasn't gotten us any closer to a resolution. Fuck this country and fuck circumstances.

My goal here today is to find out exactly what's going on beyond the political correctness and vague information we've been given. Living in the here and now is one thing, but moving forward to plan, I need the full information. I'm an American citizen, and the embassy is meant to be representing *my* rights and looking out for *my* best interests. I want to make sure they're doing that.

Now that everything is in the open and has been plastered over all the news stations, I don't need to take care and think about what I'm doing or saying. I don't need to wonder how it will affect the investigation. Whoever took Sarah would have to be living under a rock on the moon not to realize we were hunting them. They must also realize, with her face appearing all over the media, it will make it harder for them to do whatever it is they have planned. Unless, of course, they still want to ask for a ransom. At this stage, I'd pay anything to have her back.

The door opens, and I stand, expecting to see the consul general, but it's not the CG. It's George. With shoulders sagging in defeat, I let out a frustrated sigh. I close my eyes and take a deep breath in an attempt to curb my rising anger.

Is this just another example of me not being taken seriously?

"George … I was hoping to talk to the consul general. Is he coming?" I slump back down into the chair, refusing to look away from him.

"Good morning, Mrs. Johnson," he says guardedly, clearly noting my frustration. With a sigh, he moves into the room and pulls out the chair opposite me. "I'm sorry, but the consul general has a busy schedule today and couldn't cancel anything to make time for you. If you'd called ahead to make an appointment, his staff would have told you this and saved you a visit."

"What's so important that he couldn't take the time to meet with the mother of the US national who's been abducted from the country of his post? The mother whose family is currently plastered over almost every international media site?" I shout, slapping my hands onto the table between us. The action has George staring at my hands before he slowly raises his eyes back up to mine. The sadness I see in them only fuels my ire. "I don't need your sympathy, George. I need answers. I was hoping he'd give them to me."

George pushes back from the table and exhales loudly. "Yes, I can see that. To answer your question, he has a trade meeting with some dignitaries who flew in from around the region. If he could cancel, I'm sure he would. He has—as we all have—been taking Sarah's disappearance seriously, working every political angle we can to find her. We won't accept anything less than her safe return."

He removes his glasses and rubs his eyes. The black circles beneath them have been a constant for as long as I've known him. Working in diplomatic security must be consistently stressful, and US bureaucracy is filled with many political pitfalls. In realizing this, I feel a twinge of remorse at my behavior. But that quickly fades.

"The CG has also been very busy with running damage control with the UAE's vice president since the BBC aired that story two nights ago and it went viral. The Emiratis expect to have full authority over what the media does and doesn't say in this country—as you well know. Even though the story was always going to get out, we still need to minimize any political fallout to keep good relations between our two countries. It's unfortunate that this situation is being politicized."

The tone of his words lacks any accusation toward me, but they still sting.

With my jaw clenched, I briefly look away. "I can imagine. But with everyone knowing the truth now, or a version of the truth, I can't continue acting as though everything's fine and normal. It's not. I know it's the way we needed to act when we thought she'd been kidnapped, but we know her abduction is part of something bigger. I want to know what's being done to find my daughter."

George slowly shakes his head. "Jen—"

"I need to know more. I need to know how seriously our government is taking this. I need to know you're putting pressure on the Emiratis to find my daughter."

George remains stoic and watches me wipe away a stray tear from my cheek. He waits for me to regain my composure before continuing in a soft voice. "Jen, there's nothing more I can tell you. I promise we're doing everything we can. You must understand—"

I leap to my feet. "I want my daughter back!" I shout. "Is that too hard to comprehend?"

His tone and his words are nothing more than an accelerant thrown on my burning anger. I'm seething. I don't want to understand anything. I want to know what's being done. I want to be able to trust that they're doing everything they possibly can to bring Sarah back safely to me. The time for me being calm and understanding has passed. I start pacing the room again, my anger and frustration evident.

"Calm down, Mrs. Johnson. I understand what you're going—"

"You understand? You fucking understand? Have you had your daughter abducted and more than likely sold as a sex slave or child bride to one of these fucking perverts?"

I glower at George's shocked expression. He sits up straight, and his eyes flash with a look I can't discern.

"No," I continue, "I didn't think so. You don't have a fucking clue!"

"Mrs. Johnson, with all due respect, we're doing everything we can. This isn't the first abduction case I've worked on—"

I stop pacing and look at him in incredulity. "Oh, great! This has happened before. And how did that work out for you?" My sarcastic tone has him pursing his lips in response.

"Mrs. Johnson, every case is different. This is a strange one, to be sure. Kidnappings and abductions don't normally happen to Westerners in Dubai itself. Normally, they occur in other areas or countries within the region. We have our best people on it. They're reviewing the security footage, liaising with the local authorities …"

"And what are *they* doing? Sitting on their asses, reciting nursery rhymes? It's been almost three weeks. Three fucking weeks! And no one can tell me anything more than we were told after she was taken." I throw my hands in the air in frustration. Turning away from him, I press the heel of my palms into my eye sockets and take a deep breath before letting them fall to my sides. "Don't *your people* see a problem with this? The Emiratis probably know exactly where Sarah is, but they won't lift a finger to get her back. And *your people* are doing nothing about it."

George groans and shakes his head. "That's not fair. The embassy's doing everything it possibly can. Our host government has a lot riding on this as well. If we want to be bluntly honest here, your leaking this to the media has ensured that the Emiratis are focused on finding a resolution. And quickly. It has the potential to blow up and affect tourism."

"Yeah, like I'm really concerned about this country's tourism. And you know what? That's a crock. The Emiratis don't give a damn about the negative media. They get it all the time. They just pay ludicrous amounts of money to have a positive marketing campaign talk over the top of any reporting done on the realities of life here."

I start pacing again and jump on my soapbox over the hypocrisy of expat life in Dubai. "How about the way they treat tourists who come here? Come to Dubai and have a luxury five-star holiday, but don't come if you're single or you want to drink or want to go out and dance at a nightclub. What about that woman last month who was arrested because she and her boyfriend were sharing a room, and shock and horror ..." I raise my hands in the air and open my eyes wide to demonstrate my mock revulsion.

George sits back in his chair and folds his arms. With eyebrows furrowed and wearing a pinched expression, he waits out my tantrum.

"They were unmarried? Or how about the girl who got drunk at one of the hotel clubs and was raped ... and when she reported it, she was arrested for the consumption of alcohol and for having sex out of wedlock? How fair is that? Now, my daughter—a child from a married expat couple—has been abducted, and they're doing all they can? Sure. *Sure*, I really believe that."

Taking off his glasses and rubbing his face in his hand, George looks up, tired and empathetic but with no answers. The dark lines under his eyes and the shadow on his jaw show how tired he is. "Mrs. Johnson, we're doing everything we absolutely can. Navigating in these cultural waters is … challenging."

Sitting down with slumped shoulders, the brief rage that consumed me evaporates. Only sadness and fear remain. "I know. But it's not enough."

23

My lip trembles, and my eyes burn as I try to keep the tears at bay. Liam's upstairs in his room, either doing his homework or visiting his online world. If I could escape to a virtual reality where everything was as it should be, I'd be there in a heartbeat. If only life could be fixed with a few strokes on a keyboard. The problem with the virtual world, though, is you have to return at some point.

The reality of where I am hits me.

I'm a thirty-five-year-old woman living in an Arab country in the Middle East. Dubai might be a touch more progressive than the other emirates and its neighboring Gulf countries, but it's still a Muslim country based on Muslim law. Even though I'm an American national, my rights here are limited. I don't work here. I don't contribute to society in any real sense. The visa that allows me to live in this country is a spousal visa, and it's entirely dependent on Kevin and his work situation.

My conversations with both Kevin and George over the past few days replay in my mind. They're both right; we're here only at the pleasure of our host government. The rule of law I've grown up with, knowing and expecting, doesn't come into play at all, nor do the societal norms of the US. The melting pot of diverse cultures living in Dubai has created a class system. And, being near to the top of that system, it's easy to forget where you're living and the implications of being here.

Now, the blindfold has been ripped off; the false sense of security I was living under is lost. And I'm scared.

I pick up my cell phone to call Kevin and ask him to come home. I need to be held, for him to hold me. To be reassured that everything's going to be okay. I know it's asking for an outright lie, but I need to hear it so I can believe … if only for a few minutes.

I'm unlocking the screen to call Kevin when it indicates an incoming call. It's an unlisted number, and I gingerly answer it, hoping it's not a reporter or a hoax call.

"Mrs. Johnson?" The voice is deep, and his words are spoken with authority.

"Yes?" I reply cautiously, my finger hovering over the red End Call button.

"Mrs. Johnson, this is Officer Rahman with the Dubai Police. Lieutenant Ahmed has requested to meet with you and your husband this evening at headquarters."

My hand shakes as I grip the phone, securely plastering it to my ear. I listen intently to avoid any misunderstanding from his thickly accented English.

"O-okay."

"Yes, Mrs. Johnson. See you at nineteen hundred hours."

24

Chills ripple up my spine as I look around the sparsely furnished room. It's nothing more than an interview room with a clinical feel to it, not welcoming and definitely not promising. The overly bright fluorescent lighting provides the impression that this is the home of bad news and possibly sorrow, and that's not good. Not today, not when we've finally been called in by the police to hopefully get an update on Sarah's investigation. More than we've been told to date at least.

"Did the officer who called you provide any additional information other than to be here?" I ask Kevin since he also received a call to be here.

He's sitting stiffly in one of the metal chairs, reading something on his phone. The tension in the room is unmistakable.

At my question, he briefly looks up. "No. Just to be here at 7:00 p.m." His neutral tone is not unexpected, nor is his cool stare.

Kevin would be a brilliant poker player, and all his work colleagues would agree. Probably why he's been so successful in the boardroom or at closing business deals. I've been privy to this side of him, but I've never had it directed at me, and it's unnerving. Although I thought he'd be showing a bit more emotion even if it was just an eagerness to know what's going on. I secretly hope his act is for the cameras undoubtedly recording our interaction in the room, but I doubt it. It's for me.

"Okay," I respond, shaking my head.

Words are overrated. If he doesn't want to talk about why we're here, neither do I. It doesn't mean I can silence my mind from speculating. It's running through a million and one scenarios—from the serious and possible to the ludicrous and terrifying.

Have they found her? Have they arrested other people involved? Are we having our visas revoked? Did someone tell them about my stash of black-market wine? Do they have a lead, or has there been a ransom demand? Is she ... dead?

I blink away the final thoughts along with the welling tears they bring before another macabre idea comes to me.

"Do you think this has something to do with those comments by Human Rights Watch?" I stare at him, trying to gauge his reaction, absently chewing on the cuticle of a fingernail.

He stops what he's doing on his phone and drops it into his pocket before returning my stare. "Maybe. Anything's possible. Didn't you say you'd call the embassy on your way here? Do they have any idea?" He closes his eyes and leans his head against the white wall.

Him being closed off to me is frustrating. I want to scream at him, but the idea of hidden cameras stills my tongue.

"No, they don't. George said he'd been contacted for a meeting as well. So, whatever it is, it must be important." I let my gaze wander from him to a small mark on the wall at the side of his head.

Kevin's barely looked at me since we arrived. I waited in the visitor parking lot for him, too nervous to enter alone. I doubt he'd have waited for me had the situation been reversed.

"What if ... what if she's dead?" I whisper my greatest fear, which is replaying on a loop through my mind.

Kevin stands to switch seats to the one beside mine. He drapes an arm over my shoulders and pulls me to him. The smell of his aftershave comforts me as much as his arm around me. It's been too long since we've shared such an intimate moment.

"Don't think like that, Jen. You're the optimistic one. You need to believe she's fine." His words are muffled in the strands of my hair as he rests his head on my shoulder.

I let out a breath and relax into him. This is what I needed.

He thinks I'm the optimistic one? Not anymore. I'm a realist.

The embassy and Kevin's lawyer have been keeping us up-to-date with the scant information on Sarah's disappearance. My dealings have only been with the embassy—other than the one time I met the lawyer when the initial interviews and formal statements were made. Although I've had interactions with the Dubai Police on a daily basis, by design or otherwise, they really haven't shared any information on the investigation. Our updates have been mainly from George at the embassy.

We never really expected more from the police. We were warned at the beginning that this was how it would probably be. As long as they were doing their job with the investigation, it shouldn't matter that their communication skills were lacking. But refusing outright to take our calls or answer our questions feels like a breach of our rights. Of course, we have no rights. We're only visitors to the country, American, and white—the trio of badness. Being called in tonight—for who knows what—has conjured up a myriad of emotions and concerns.

"*A-salaamu aleikom.* Mr. Johnson and Mrs. Johnson, it is good that you could come in today."

I recognize the deep lilt and stilted English belonging to the Dubai Police commissioner. His blue dress uniform is fresh with seams as sharp as the knife sitting in his belt next to his gun holster. Boots that could normally double as a mirror are covered with a slight film of sand. He presents a menacing figure, giving credence to his reputation as a no-nonsense official. Pity his reputation also includes expat hating and ruthlessness. We've been warned repeatedly to watch what we say to him. He's known to take a literal translation to everything said and doesn't take kindly to sarcasm or jokes made against his country or his religion.

Behind him, to his right, stands Lieutenant Ahmed.

"Yes. We came in as soon as your officer contacted us," Kevin says, standing to offer his hand to the police commissioner.

"Good, good. This is good. Please sit down." He nods, ignoring Kevin's hand and taking a seat at the head of the conference table. "My staff has reviewed all the evidence, and what we have here is definitely an abduction made by a group who is involved in people smuggling and human trafficking."

Although there's a manila folder in front of him, he doesn't bother to open it or refer to it. I casually try to get a glance at what it says and am disappointed that the labels on the front are in Arabic. No English at all, not even a reference to our name. The case file, if it is one, might not even be ours or anything relevant to this case. Judging by the way he looks us over and is addressing us, it probably isn't.

"From what we have found out, your daughter was taken and moved out of the Emirates immediately. There was no involvement of any Emirati citizen in this. It was instigated purely by outsiders … a group of South Asians, we believe. We have the two who are under suspicion of being involved in custody. And they will be dealt with under our laws." There's a pregnant pause before he continues. "Now that the investigation has moved outside our jurisdiction, we are formally closing the case."

"Wh-what? Why?" I grip Kevin's hand under the table and look between him and the police commissioner.

Kevin's face has blanched, but he remains silent.

The police commissioner narrows his eyes at me for the interruption before he continues. "It is as I have explained, Mrs. Johnson. This case no longer has anything to do with the United Arab Emirates. Was a crime committed? Yes. We have investigated and have two collaborators in custody. The crime was done by outsiders, and our investigation has found that your daughter is no longer in the country. Because of this, we will not spend any more time or resources on this case. We will close it. It will be known that it has been closed, and the United Arab Emirates is not an instigator or involved in the abduction. We will provide a briefing to Interpol on the request of the American Embassy and continue to provide assistance if needed. But, as far as we are concerned, we have done all we can. *Halas*. Finished."

"No, you can't …" I start, but Kevin's firm squeeze on my hand and pointed look have me swallowing my words.

The police commissioner stands and walks toward the door.

As far as he's concerned, this is it; it's finished, finalized. *Halas*.

My mind is having difficulty understanding why this is the end for the investigation. *How can it be the end? How can they close it when we still have no idea where Sarah is or who has her?*

I look up at him as he speaks again. "We will be issuing a statement to the press now. Come. They will need to see you standing with me to send the correct message."

I sit motionless in my chair. Frozen. The brilliance of the lights burns my eyes as I try to blink back the tears. Only the warmth leached from Kevin's closeness keeps me from becoming hysterical as he gently pulls me up and directs me toward the door. Lieutenant Ahmed holds the door open and follows us out of the room.

I'm shaking. Kevin's arms wrapped around my shoulders provide much-needed support as we walk down the corridor, following the police commissioner. He opens the door and ushers us through. The setup is similar to that of the US Consulate, except, instead of a lectern on a dais, we are ushered to chairs behind a table.

My vision blurs, and my head throbs with the assault of the bright lights. Breaths come short and fast as I stare blindly out at the media seated in front of us. It doesn't have the same chaotic feel as the last press conference we attended. There's more order and calm. I can't stand it. I just can't …

Kevin's arms tighten around me as I place a hand over my eyes and cry.

25

———

"There's so much darkness in the world. You don't realize until it touches you. What's happened is by far one of the most heart-wrenching … I just can't … I can't even imagine trying to hold the pain that you must be carrying." Melanie sits beside me by the pool, legs dangling in the water.

"She's my daughter, and I've failed her." My arms wrap around my body, hands gripping hard. The sobs arrive unasked, and I don't bother holding them in. There's no need to keep up appearances. Not that I could anyway. After what feels like an ambush instigated by the police with their press conference, I've been slowly losing my sanity.

Melanie sighs. "I know, Jen. I know. You can't do anything to change what's happened, but you do need to look forward—"

"I can't just forget and move on. I refuse to believe this is the end." I rock back and forth, breaths becoming short and rapid.

Melanie brings me in for a hug, and as my tears mark her clothes, I find myself thinking of my husband, my partner in life. It should be him providing me comfort.

Am I a bad wife to be glad he's not?

He excused himself earlier to go and smooth things over with the lawyers at the office. I should be thankful that he comforted me when the world dropped from beneath us. At least he came home after the police's so-called press conference to help me break the news to Liam.

"I know that, but you need to be smart about this. You need to look forward and work out the best way for you to do that. Think strategic. Think long-term. The government and authorities here have made it abundantly clear that they're not going to help. Sure, they've closed the case, but you need a plan." Melanie pauses for a second before continuing on in a softer tone. "What does Kevin think?"

Her gentle words break through the manic state of my mind. I sit up and sniffle as I scrub the tears from my face with the bottom of my shirt. I can't bear to look at her as I divulge some of Kevin's company's secrets. Secrets that show how intricately the government is involved in our affairs and how they have been manipulating our behavior.

"Kevin's toeing the party line. His company took a lot of grief from the government after the media fallout. They've been monitoring the firm pretty closely since the abduction, and he's been told if he steps out of line, all the company's assets will be frozen, and their business license will be suspended." I look at my friend as she sits beside me in shock. "The government started reviewing personnel files, looking at visas, and HR was forced to refile their business license."

"You've got to be kidding," she says incredulously.

We both know that this sort of thing happens. It's another one of those unspoken scenarios people whisper about behind closed doors. Like when the government freezes bank accounts once a visa expires or is revoked. Urban myths of expats caught up in a vicious cycle when trying to repatriate and liquidate their assets. Vehicles that can't be sold until the loan for them is paid out in full, which is impossible with accounts having been frozen to stop funds from being transferred out of the country. None of it makes sense. Tales are told of cars being left, stranded in the airport parking lot, furniture left in houses, and family pets driven to the desert or just left in the street to fend for themselves. The ugly underbelly that can turn any expat's five-star experience into a living nightmare. Much like mine has become.

I pick up some leaves from the paved area beside me and start pulling them apart before throwing the pieces in the pool. The filter's running, and the bits of debris float with the water flow to the deep end before disappearing into the catchment box. "The government was very upset about the media accusations saying they'd let this happen and that they weren't doing enough to solve the case. Once that happened … well, you saw what they did tonight. Closed the case and passed the torch to Interpol and Human Rights Watch. The very people they told us not to talk to in the first place! Made themselves look like the shining white knights, talking about all the effort that they'd put into finding Sarah and emphasizing that it was instigated by non-Emiratis. They've tied our hands and prevented us from chasing any leads ourselves."

"But that's just here in Dubai, isn't it?"

"Yes. We can't ask any questions or follow any leads here, in Dubai." I shake my head in frustration. It's hard, coming to grips with all of this.

"What are you going to do?"

"I-I really don't know. Hiring a private security company is a no go unless we can give them more leads to chase down. Unfortunately, they're pretty much only good for bodyguard services. They can't operate within the UAE anyway, which is what I meant by us not being able to privately investigate or chase leads here." I sigh and rub my eyes.

I'm exhausted. The whirlwind of emotions over the past few weeks have caused havoc to my health. I can't remember the last time I was able to get a good night's sleep that wasn't aided by alcohol or pharmaceuticals.

"I have a meeting at the embassy tomorrow. They've been talking with the State Department since the BBC ran that damn interview. With everything that's going on politically back home, they're now wanting to help."

As Melanie pulls her feet out of the warm water to sit cross-legged, I smile and think of our first summer here. The kids were excited to have a pool in the backyard, and they were constantly out here. The heated water during summer inspired them to add bubble bath near the water jets—two bottles of it. The ensuing mess it created was enough for the polite South Asian pool boy to lose his temper. He keeps the pool overly chlorinated now to stop any silliness. Not that there's been any silliness around the pool for quite some time. I sniff back a tear at the memory of happier times.

"I keep thinking about what we've done and what we've been doing over the past few weeks. At every turn, we've been told to keep our mouths shut and let the authorities handle it. We haven't had any transparency whatsoever with the Emiratis' investigation. I was optimistic in the beginning because the surveillance they set up was extensive. I kept thinking they'd be able to track Sarah and get her back for us. But they haven't, and too much time has passed now to do anything else. Diplomatically, the US government has their hands tied, and from what I've seen, they've only provided limited assistance." I run my fingers through my hair and voice a fear that's been playing on my mind as of late. "Do you think we should have done more … spoken out sooner?"

She leans back on her arms and looks to the sky as she lets out a lengthy exhale. "To be honest, no. You couldn't have predicted what was going to happen. And I strongly believe that, had you caused any waves, you probably would have been in a jail cell right now or extradited back home. I think all the advice our government has given you is sound. It's just … I don't know … unfortunate."

I scoff at Melanie's words. "Unfortunate?"

She looks over at me and offers a small smile. "Sorry, poor choice of words. I agree; the Dubai Police should have resolved this weeks ago, and I'm desperately sorry you don't know more on what went wrong."

"Yes. You know, Mel," I ask slowly, deciding to air the main reason I asked her to come over tonight after Kevin left, "I'm thinking of going back home, back to the US. Do you think that's cowardly of me? Do you think Sarah will think I've given up on her if we move back home?"

Melanie's response is instantaneous. "No, not at all. I don't know how you've been staying sane at all with the reminders of everything around you."

The *muezzin*'s strident voice rings out from the loudspeakers of the mosque behind our villa, calling the faithful to prayer, letting us know that the night is creeping in. I struggle with my current thoughts, but I can't think of another way to move forward.

I lie back on the warm brick pavers and stare at the sky. Taking a measured breath, I repeat my concerns to the stars. "I don't know what I can do from this country to help Sarah."

"Have you spoken to Kevin about this yet?" Melanie's voice is cautious.

I know she senses the struggles we're having.

I shake my head and add a cynical laugh. "I haven't talked to Kevin about much at all lately. He hasn't been around. And I just don't get it. What father would stay away from his family during a crisis like this?"

Melanie mirrors my pose by lying back. Her pursed lips and furrowed brow tell me I'm not alone with my current thoughts on Kevin.

"He blames me, you know. He hates me for it," I whisper.

"I'm sure that's not true."

"It is." I sigh, looking at the patch of stars in the darkness. "He told me as much. I think me going back to the US might help things between us, as warped as that sounds. To Kevin, I'm a constant reminder of all of the mistakes."

Melanie sits up and twists her body to face me. Seeing she has my full attention, she speaks. "He doesn't blame you. Those words were spoken in frustration and anger. Sure, he shouldn't have said them. He could have thought a bit more about his timing and delivery. Who knows why he's been acting irrational lately? But everyone deals with loss differently. I don't agree with the way he's been handling it all, but I at least am trying to understand." She swipes a few errant wisps of hair from her face. "You two are the worst with communicating at the best of times, but the stakes have never been so high. If you ask me, I think the two of you need to get away from here and reconnect, both with Liam and as a family. Take away all the outside influences of work, school, police ... and just work through it."

We sit and stare at each other for a minute. Melanie's insight and understanding of everything I've been going through, everything my family's been going through, are both timely and warranted. She's right. If I let the situation continue along the path the external forces are pushing it toward, it will have disastrous consequences for me and my family. And that's regardless of whether Sarah is found or not.

Or not.

Two words ... I can't afford to mutter those two words regarding Sarah's safe return.

The main actors influencing the outcome don't care about me or my family. They care about their jobs, their political standing, their own countries. Not about me. Not my family. They are driven by the monetary costs, conflicting priorities, and the time to invest in the search. I can't trust them to look out for me and my family, not now. If we continue letting them guide us and gag us, we'll get nowhere. Kevin and I need to unite and work through other options and move forward. But we need to reconnect first and to forgive each other.

"I think you're right," I say through a sigh. "If this tears us apart, I don't know what I'll do."

It's the sort of thing you hear about. How a family can be ripped apart in the aftermath of tragedy. The way Kevin and I are spiraling out of sync with each other puts us directly on that path. Melanie's right. I need a plan.

"I've been trying so hard to keep it all together. To pretend to the outside world that everything's fine. Telling half-truths about what's happened and about the investigation. Being the dutiful expat, wife, and mom, keeping up appearances. All for what?" I rake my fingers through my hair, sucking in a deep breath before exhaling it loudly. I'm exhausted. "I have a son whose only life outside of school is some virtual world he's created. A husband who's pulling away more and more every single day and whose priorities between his work and family have become muddled. I'm suffocating. Imagine living in the middle of the desert with nothing but space and feeling suffocated? Every time I hear the call to prayer or see a woman wearing an *abaya*, I'm reminded of where we are and what Sarah might be subjected to. It's as though my breath is being ripped out of me."

Looking up at the stars, I could be anywhere. Anywhere.

"Summer was only a few short weeks ago. The freedom we take for granted is just ... as long as we're here, it's lost, gone. I need to leave this place. I need to go home." There's a profound sadness to my words, and they press heavily against my chest.

"Yes, you've said that."

"I know, but I'm totally serious now. I'm thinking I should just pack up and leave." I sit up and look at Melanie once more.

It's as though the weight has been lifted from me. For the first time in weeks, maybe even longer, I feel free from a burden I didn't realize was pressing down on me. I could be anywhere; it wouldn't change the circumstances. Why should I stay in a country where I'm constantly being watched? I'd be able to create more awareness and be more helpful in a supportive environment. A known environment.

Home.

Melanie's eyes widen, and she takes my hand. "Jen, I don't think you should make any hasty decisions."

"I don't think I'm being hasty. I think the writing has been on the wall for a while. I'm just now reading it. There's nothing I can do here. Heck, you just agreed with me on that five minutes ago. Sarah isn't here. I can't look for her here. If not here, then why not at home where I can at least have the freedom to deal with everything the way we should be?"

With a new sense of direction and hope, I stand and head inside for coffee. Time to retake control. Time to sober up and devise a plan. "Yes, I need to talk to the embassy tomorrow and run through my options. The State Department has a higher involvement now. I need to find out what I should do and if I can do it from home. And I need to talk to Kevin. He's got to agree."

26

———

The meeting at the embassy went surprisingly well. They agreed that not much more could be achieved by my staying here that couldn't be done in the US. I don't think it was my imagination either that the consul general, who finally had the time to see me, was relieved.

Before I left, George and I sat down together, and he gave me a list of contacts for various people back home. It was quite extensive, and I was happy to see the names of various non-governmental organizations and lobbyists as well as contact details for people at both the State Department and the White House.

As I haven't seen Kevin since yesterday and he hasn't been returning my calls, I'm going to track him down myself. The embassy wants us to sign some documents that provide information to Interpol, and the sooner they get them back, the better.

I'm in his office building, and it's with trepidation as the elevator doors to the twelfth-floor office space open. Sarah's abduction has affected the staff here in one way or another. If it wouldn't generate such negative publicity, I'm certain the big bosses would've fired Kevin or transferred him back to the US weeks ago. But with the local investigation closed, I'm sure everything will start to calm down, and business will return to normal. It's just the way of doing business in the Middle East—continuing to put out fires and then moving on.

After taking a deep breath, I step out of the elevator and onto the plush carpet and nod to the receptionist sitting behind the desk across from me. Her job is effectively to act as a guard dog, making sure only authorized personnel come onto the floor. She also holds the key to the locked doors behind her, providing entrance to the office space itself.

"Good morning, Mrs. Johnson. I'm sorry about your daughter. Any updates?"

The hesitant look of sympathy on her face twists my stomach into knots. I should be used to the look by now, but I'm not.

"Hi, Mandy. No, nothing new. I'm here to see Kevin. We seem to keep missing each other. He needs to review some documents. It's all a bit time-sensitive." I offer her a small smile and stand next to the door that will give me access to their workspace once she unlocks it for me.

"Of course, Mrs. Johnson. He should be in his office." She reaches under her desk to press the button that unlocks the door.

Its quiet buzz is all I need to hear before I pull it open and step through.

"Mrs. Johnson?" Mandy says quietly.

I stop in the archway and turn toward her.

"I'm very, very sorry. You don't deserve any of this. I'll pray for you and your family."

"Thank you, Mandy," I say, fighting back tears before heading down the hallway.

Maybe not all the company's staff is as annoyed with the fallout as Kevin alluded to.

I pass a few other staff members on my way to Kevin's corner office, some walking around and others sitting behind their cubicle workstations in the open-plan section of the office. Most give me a small smile as they hurry by. A few seem rather alarmed by my presence and shoot furtive glances my way. I'm sure they think I'm unhinged; some of the media coverage has certainly portrayed me as that. Kevin's need to spend more time at the office than at home, supporting me, could also have them gossiping and jumping to conclusions.

I stop in front of Kevin's door and take another deep breath.

I barely register that the screens on his glass windows are closed in privacy mode before I open the door and step into his office, only to come to a complete halt.

Oh my God.

Standing before me, Kevin and Jacquie are locked in an embrace—and not the quick embrace of a friend either. Her head rests on his chest, and his is bent forward, resting on the top of hers, arms wrapped around each other. Their eyes are closed, and they have yet to notice my entrance.

The shock is absolute. Before I realize what I'm doing, I swing up the hand holding my cell phone and snap a photo. The camera's loud shutter attracts their attention, and they both look up at me. The horror and guilt on their faces is all I need to know that my initial thoughts and fears were correct.

Kevin is the first to react, lowering his arms and stepping away from Jacquie. He takes a step toward me, raising his hands as though I were a skittish animal about to take off. "It's not what it looks like, Jen."

"Really? And what do you think it looks like?" I look at his work acquaintance, the one who I've never really called a friend but has been part of our social circle.

She has yet to raise her head to look at me. I'd like to think she's hanging her head in shame until she finally looks up, and I see the indignation in her eyes.

"Kevin," she starts, her tone condescending, "let's not coddle her. There's been too much coddling as of late. I'm sick of playing second fiddle whenever she goes into some manic spin. You've done nothing wrong."

Her words confuse me, but as I look between them both, bewildered, I want answers. "Huh? So, what exactly is going on here? Please, enlighten me. By no means do I want to be *coddled*."

I narrow my eyes at Kevin as he scrubs his forehead with his hand and turns to Jacquie.

"Jacquie, now isn't the time."

My head tilts to the side.

Now isn't the time?

What does that mean?

My mind is still trying to process what I'm seeing. I know what's going on, and in the deep, dark recesses of my mind, I suppose I've considered this as a possibility.

And me, having a manic spin? What does that even mean?

Kevin looks at her with so much tenderness, I snap. "What the fuck is going on?"

Both look up to me at my sharp words, but Jacquie talks first.

"I love him," she says without apology. "We've been seeing each other for a while now, and we believe it's serious. He was waiting for the right time to tell you, but with … Sarah's disappearance, there hasn't been a right time."

Kevin starts pacing as I slump into the chair by the door.

I go over the words in my mind.

Sarah's disappearance … not the right time.

That means, this has been going on for a while. Their affair isn't new. I close my eyes and review the last twelve months. The late nights, trips away, eagerness for the kids and me to spend the summer in the US. The small touches and secret looks and smiles between them that I excused as the innocent intimacy of good friends, work colleagues.

How could I have been so stupid?

A small click brings me out of my reverie, and I look up to see that Kevin has closed and locked the door. Something I'm sure he's regretting he didn't do earlier. He looks at me, mixed emotions racing across his face. Frustration, anger, fear ... but no regret. I don't see regret in his eyes. I think he's sorry I'm here and that I've finally discovered the reason for his behavior and treatment of me, but I don't think he's sorry for whatever *this* is between them.

"I'm sorry, Jen. I didn't mean for you to find out like this. There's just been so much going on. Fuck!"

I scoff at his half-assed apology.

He sits across from me, running a hand through his hair. "I don't know what to say. Jacquie has been helping me deal with all of this. There's been pressure from work, and the government has been fucking me around ..."

I don't want to hear their pitiful excuses. Whatever reason they've conjured to justify this betrayal, they can keep it. Whatever narrative they tell each other to make them feel better and deny their guilt, I'm not interested. I need air and a drink. I can't be here right now. With renewed energy and focus, I stand and pull the envelope from my bag and offer it to Kevin, wishing they were divorce papers and not consent forms for a memorandum of understanding—an MOU—between us, Interpol, and the embassy.

"I don't want to get into this right now. Sign these papers and have them couriered to George or one of his staff at the embassy. They're urgent." I turn to look at my husband's mistress. "I don't expect to see you again, Jacquie. Don't call, and don't come around. Stay away from Liam, and stay away from me."

I unlock the door and leave the office. The pity stares from the office staff are there, but I can't work out if they are pitying me because my daughter is still missing or because my husband is a cheating asshole. It's probably the latter.

I exit the secure part of the office space and reach the elevators where Mandy is still stationed at her desk. She looks up as I walk past her and hit the elevator's call button. Considering she has a desk in the waiting area, she ought to have a remote for it behind her desk. Maybe she does. Maybe I'm in such a hurry to leave and be anywhere else that I preempted her and left her bereft of her duties.

"I could've gotten that for you, Mrs. Johnson." She sits up straight, hands gently resting on the desk.

There's a sharpness in her eyes that prompts me to ask a question I'm not ready to have answered yet. "Did you know about him and Jacquie?"

"Yes, I did." I watch her carefully as she answers. She doesn't move; she doesn't blink.

"How long?" I ask, looking away from her to watch the numbers creep up on the screen above the elevator. It's something I know I'll regret asking, but I'm curious to find out when the staff here in the office became aware.

"Twelve months, give or take," she says softly with a hint of apology.

The elevator beeps to announce the arrival of the car that's my lift to somewhere other than here. The betrayal of the one person in the world who is supposed to have my back cuts. The fact that he's not even remorseful or contrite cuts twice as deep. The realization that it's been going on throughout our ordeal might as well be a knife through my heart.

27

———

Twelve months.

They've been seeing each other for twelve months.

The business trips, late-night client meetings … how much of it was a lie? The insistence for us to return to the US for summer break to spend time with family—was it just a ruse to get us out of the picture so he could spend more time with Jacquie? God, were they sleeping in my bed?

The last thought makes me want to vomit.

I tip my wineglass and gulp down the remaining liquid before pouring myself another. I consider drinking it straight from the bottle, but I think of Liam locked away in his room, playing in his virtual world, and I push it away.

He's old enough to understand what something like this means, and it's going to devastate him. He's already withdrawn and moody, more so than what's deemed normal for a typical teenager even though he's only twelve. According to his counselor, Sarah's abduction has affected him so much that he's exhibiting extreme antisocial behavior. He's drowning in guilt and anger toward himself and projecting it onto anyone who tries to reach out to him. It's something I didn't notice.

Other than the keeping to himself and staying in his room, he seems normal to me. Maybe I just haven't been paying attention. Maybe I've been so wrapped up in my own guilt and anger with what's happened and how we've been treated, I just thought he'd be okay. Or is it because we're kindred spirits? Being at ground zero through all this allows us to *get* each other and excuse each other's behavior. Considering the circumstances, I think he's fine.

But I don't want to think about how he's going to react when he finds out his father has been slowly ripping apart the seams of this family. More so than the jagged seams Sarah's abduction has made. As a family, we've failed Liam and more than likely given him a life sentence of therapy.

The slamming of a door echoes down the quiet hallway. It's a few minutes before the telltale cadence of Kevin's shoes click on the tiles, heading in my direction. After all the recent absences and today's revelations, I wasn't sure if he'd come home tonight or even come back at all.

I lick my lips and make a conscious effort to stop tapping my foot on the carpet. I'm nervous about the conversation we're about to have. The liquid courage sits uncomfortably in my stomach, chastising me for drinking the last glass of wine. I shouldn't be drinking. If anything, I've learned over the past few weeks that alcohol doesn't make you forget or heal a broken heart. It just masks the symptoms temporarily and makes you feel twice as bad from the guilt of it.

I can't decide whether to sit or stand when he enters the room. He must know I'll be waiting to confront him. With everything that's happened over the past few weeks, I'm not sure I'm ready to deal with his infidelity as well. This has a definite feel about it. It's as though I'm caught up in one of those dark fairy tales that never has a happily ever after. Knowing my luck, I've been cast as the sacrificial character who needs to be destroyed or beaten down so the others can have their happily ever afters. From the moment I caught Kevin and *her* in the middle of their embrace, my escape from this place and the fresh start I so desperately wanted has taken on a completely different meaning.

Kevin enters the room and walks straight to the armoire, ignoring my presence. His back is to me, and I'm able to silently watch him pour himself a whisky.

This man has given me so much. He's given me the life I could never have dreamed of. Laughter and love that's spanned time zones and cultures. True adventures that people would rarely dare to put on their bucket list. We've visited both the ancient wonders and natural wonders of the world. The ancient city of Petra where Liam rode beside us on a donkey as we explored the ruins in all their crumbling magnificence. The holy city of Jerusalem where we had the children baptized and observed the nexus of and divisions between the three great Abrahamic religions. We've dived alongside wondrous sea life on the Great Barrier Reef and watched the sun set over the top of Uluru in Australia's interior. This man, who's never forgotten a birthday or an anniversary, gifted me with two wonderful children. Until recently, my life read like a real-life fairy tale.

I can't help it when my eyes tear up as I look at this man who has given me so much for so long. He's loved me with such passion and determination. I thought our story would continue forever.

But it won't.

There'll be no coming back from this.

Kevin turns with his glass in hand and leans against the armoire. It sickens me that he's standing there, acting all casual, as if he doesn't have a care in the world. As if our lives aren't in tatters and his latest betrayal isn't the unwanted fuel he threw on the existing inferno.

He looks at me with scorn; there's no affection in his eyes. It's in contrast to the expression of guilt he had in his office earlier when I caught him in the act. I suppose, in that moment, he felt guilty. Guilty for being caught. Sorry he couldn't control the narrative into something he could spin or manipulate me into believing that everything was my fault. As I study him, I see no remorse. He's back to being the man who blames me for our missing daughter.

"How could you, Kevin?" I blurt out, not being able to stand the silence or the scorn. "How could you do this to us, to your family?"

"It's not something I did consciously to hurt anyone. It just happened." The words belie both his demeanor and expression. Sounding apologetic, but he's not. His tone offers no apology.

I purse my lips and briefly look away with a shake of my head. Tears threaten to fall, but I refuse to let them. I need strength now.

"I can't keep living like this. I can't keep doing the same things, pretending nothing's wrong," I say, speaking softly as I stare out of the window, refusing to look at him. My words speak more about the situation with Sarah than his infidelity. It's just another nail, another thing to add to our problems.

"Nobody's asking you to pretend." His words are filled with contempt and a touch of venom.

I look at him in disbelief. His expression is closed off. I can't believe he thinks this.

"But that's just it. Nobody's asking anything of me. All I get is pity from those who can be bothered. Everyone else, well, they've all just moved on, and I can't. I see Sarah everywhere … when I take Liam to school, at the breakfast table, in the media room. I miss her so much. I just expect her to be there. I want her to be there. It makes me sad. But, now, knowing about you and Jacquie, my eyes are wide open, and I'm so angry." I take a deep breath and try to calm my growing rage. My words are passionate, and I'm all but shouting at him. But seeing him so emotionless, it spurs me on. "And I'm pissed, Kevin. I'm so pissed. In a matter of a few weeks, I've lost my daughter and my husband. I don't know what I'm meant to do with that. I don't know how I'm meant to move on from that. My whole entire world has been ripped away from me. It's imploded, and I just don't know how to get over it."

I sit down as my anger dissipates. I don't want it to, but I'm just too tired. Tired of fighting, tired of wondering what's going to happen next. When Kevin says nothing, I continue more softly. "You betrayed me, Kevin. You've fucking ruined me. I'm assuming that, as you didn't want to go to grief counseling with me, you don't want to go to marriage counseling either."

Kevin chuckles to himself as he takes a sip of his drink. I know the answer before the words escape his lips. "No, I don't."

Asshole.

It's hard to gain a victory in a battle you didn't know you were a part of. By coming late to the fight, all the standard weapons and strategies that could be used to work this out are useless. I want to ask how he could give up on us. To know what I did or didn't do that was so colossal that it drove him into another woman's arms. Or what Jacquie did or said to have lured him away. But, with everything else going on, I'm just exhausted.

"Do you have any intention of trying to work on our marriage?" I ask, wanting to know and not at all amused that he finds this situation humorous.

"No," he deadpans and takes another mouthful of his drink. His eyes hold a touch of sadness, and for a minute, I want to know what's put it there.

But it's too late. I don't think I can deal with this anymore. My fight for him, for us, has left me. I need to conserve my energy for the fight for my survival because that's what this is going to turn into.

I slouch over and rub my fingers through my hair. This is it. I have no other option left to me. "I'm going back to the US, and I want a divorce."

Kevin chortles. I have no idea why he's finding all of this comical. But when I look at him, all I see is a twisted look of disgust on his face aimed at me.

"Sure. You want to go back to the US? Go for it. I'm not going to stop you. Yes to the divorce as well. I couldn't agree more." He takes another sip of his drink, never breaking eye contact.

I'm like an animal caught in a game of cat and mouse, except he's the hunter and I'm his prey.

"So—"

Before I can finish my thoughts, he pounces. "But you're not taking Liam."

"What?" I blink and sit up straight.

Not take Liam? How can he suggest that?

The thought that Liam wouldn't come with me never even crossed my mind. Not only is Liam dealing with losing his sister, but he will also have to deal with his cheating father and the implications of how that will play out with us as a family. Dubai has shown her true dark underbelly, and I don't want Liam to have any part of it. At least at home, we can start fresh without any of the reminders, any of the taint.

"You heard me. You're not taking Liam with you. He can stay here with me." Kevin turns and tops off his glass. He's acting like he's talking about the weather, not the fact that he's stripping my world and my identity from me.

"What?" I repeat incredulously.

Is he insane? As if I would leave Liam here, alone to fend for himself. *Who does he think will look after Liam? The housemaid? Or is he planning on playing happy family with his mistress?* That thought makes the wine sitting in my stomach churn with unease.

He turns, giving me a once-over. I'm on my feet now, teeth clenched so hard that my cheeks are aching. His lips turn up into a slight grimace when he realizes I'm going to challenge him.

What did he think I'd do? My family is being torn apart, and he thinks I'm just going to walk away and … do what? Start over?

"You're the reason my daughter was in a position to be taken, and you think I'd trust you with my son? I've no intention of moving back to the US. There are too many opportunities here, and now, all the pressure's off the company from the government. Leaving would be professional suicide." He shakes his head. "The schools are better here. Liam should stay. And, to be honest, he'd be better off here with me."

My mouth opens as I try to comprehend his words.

Before I can offer a rebuttal, he continues. "I can't trust you anymore, Jen. I don't trust you at all. The way I see it, you have two choices. You can go back to the US and start a new life. By yourself. Or I'll *let* you stay here, and you can be a part of Liam's life."

"You fucking bastard! How dare you! How could you do this to me after all the years we've been married? After all we've gone through?" I spit out in anger.

"It's simple. I can't ever forgive you for what you've done. I can't look at you and not think about what's happened. I wholeheartedly blame you for my daughter's abduction …" Kevin's facade crumbles, and I can see the pain on his face at the thought of Sarah. He's punishing me for Sarah, for putting her in a position for her to be taken. "For her being sold into slavery or prostitution—assuming she's still alive. You're not going to be given the opportunity to do that to another child."

"She's not just your daughter," I whisper almost inaudibly.

I sympathize with the grief he feels over Sarah. I feel it, too, but I'll be damned if I let him punish me for it. Sarah's abduction, as much as I feel the guilt, is not my fault. I can't be held accountable for it. It's the authorities in this country who turn a blind eye to the people trafficking, the whoring, and the underground criminal networks that allowed this to happen.

"I'll fight you over this. You know that, right? You do realize the courts almost always rule for the child to stay with the mother, and with your infidelity … you don't stand a chance."

Kevin lets out a sardonic laugh and runs a hand through his hair. "Remember where you are, Jen. You're not in the US now. Who do you think the local courts will appoint custody of my son to? You don't have any rights in the family court here. If we go to court, we'll see how long the UAE government lets you stay. Without a spousal visa, they'll kick you out of the country. If that's the way you want to play it, go for it."

My body is shaking. I can't believe he would threaten me like this. I could kick myself for thinking he'd make this easy.

"As it is, I have his passport. You won't be taking him anyway. On legal advice, I've alerted the embassy and immigration that Liam can't leave the country without permission from both parents. If you try to leave, it'll come up in the system, saying he can't travel, and you'll be taken into custody." He looks proud of himself as he says this. As though I should give him a gold star for being so thorough in his destruction of my life.

When did he get a chance to set all this up? I only saw him this morning; his affair only came to light earlier today.

"You wouldn't do that," I whisper, trying to keep my emotions under control.

I can't believe his disdain for me runs so deep that he's prepared to take these measures. Legal advice … it hits me who provided it.

That bitch.

I don't know what I did for him to seek the comfort of another woman's arms, but until Sarah's disappearance, I wouldn't have thought he was capable of such vindictiveness. Until Sarah's disappearance, I thought we were happy. But ever since she was taken, all I've seen is his disappointment and his growing anger toward me.

"It's already done," he says with sad eyes.

He looks down to the floor, as though he were inspecting his shoes, and I watch as he closes his eyes and takes a deep breath.

Maybe he's having second thoughts?

"No. You can't do this." I shake my head in disbelief.

He looks up to me. The sadness has been replaced by a steely determination. "Look at where you are, Jen. This sort of thing happens all the time. You have no idea."

I sit back down, defeated. That's the thing. I do know what goes on here, in this country and in this region. I might not see how it all plays out from the perspective of a businessman, but I've seen the effects on the school playground. Dubai—the great melting pot of cultures. A place where East meets West and lives in harmony—until they don't.

The local legal system reflects tribal customs in regard to men being given more authority within the system. It's not a religious thing, as many might be quick to conclude. It's because the UAE is a patriarchal society where males are given preference in both custom and law. So, when Kevin says this sort of stuff happens all the time, I know exactly what he means. Although it doesn't excuse his behavior and his role in imposing it on me.

"What are you thinking? What's happened to you?" I ask, wondering aloud where my loving and caring husband of sixteen years has gone. "You asshole. I can't believe you, you … asshole."

Kevin looks at me and smiles, but it's more of a grimace, and it doesn't reach his eyes. "Maybe I am. But I meant what I said."

He walks out of the room, leaving me and my shredded heart behind.

28

———

The wind blows softly through my hair as I gaze out over the expanse of nothingness. Just rolling sand dunes shimmering in the setting sun. The air movement causes a subtle shift of the landscape as the grains of sand vibrate against each other. I once thought this arid place was beautiful, majestic even. A part of me loved the concept of this barren wasteland, imagining what it would've been like to live during the era when adventure was rife and Arabian tales were less myth and legend and more reality.

I feel the tears rolling down my cheeks. A strong gust of wind would plaster the sand to my face, adding a cruel dimension to my sorrow. Another example of how this desert can turn something pure and meaningful into something so harsh and unpleasant.

"We used to enjoy coming out here, camping. We'd bring out the firewood and build a fire after the sun went down. It was serene, peaceful even." I scrub the tears away and give Melanie a sad smile. "You know, we'd get takeout and bring it with us. It was so much easier than packing camping rations. Less hassle and cleanup."

Melanie nods her understanding. She's beside her truck, leaning up against the door. She knows the importance of why we're here.

I bend to pick up a handful of sand before standing again.

"Sarah hated camping," I admit out loud. "She hated the sand. There's no getting away from it. It's in the car, the tent, the sleeping bag, your clothes. It's different from camping in a forest or national park somewhere. You can keep the dirt away, you know? But the sand? No chance. It gets in where you don't want it. No escaping it."

With my hands cupped in front of my body, I watch the sun set beyond the distant dunes. It *is* peaceful. As the wind gently picks up, I extend my arms in front and rotate my wrists. The sand falls and scatters under the command of the breeze. The movement is gentle, appearing orchestrated by a silent symphony, with each granule of sand being conducted to its resting place.

Mesmerized by its movement, I contemplate how the Bedouin people managed to navigate across this desert. The UAE has one of the largest sand deserts that stretches from the Arabian Gulf coast to the Empty Quarter and east to the Hajjar Mountains. With countless intricate dunes, the Bedouin used the stars and the sun to navigate. It's not surprising that, before GPS, people could get lost for days or weeks out here. Plenty died out here. For all its external beauty, the desert is a death trap to the unprepared. The brutality of it exposes despair on the mind, as the sand's ability to penetrate everything gives it dominance over all else.

"With every passing day, the chances of finding her decreases. No one's looking anymore. Interpol has all the information, but the trail's gone cold. It's been cold for weeks, and the Emiratis just doesn't want to admit it to us. Sarah's just another face to add to the pile."

I pick up another handful of sand, only to watch it blow away.

The darkness slowly rolls across, swallowing the last of the sun's rays. It's as silent as it is deadly. Without the warmth of a fire, the temperature drop is almost instant.

"We waited too long and relied too heavily on the Dubai Police to find and retrieve Sarah. Maybe if we'd hired someone in the beginning, like a private security company or something, we'd be in front of the game. Kevin tried to hire someone, but it was too late." I shake my head, thinking of all the wrong decisions we made. The trust we put in the wrong people. "When we thought her abduction was a kidnapping, it seemed that everyone and everything we needed was already sitting in the front room to our villa. How wrong we were."

The disappearing heat cools the sweat on my body. The resulting chill vibrates down my spine, and I zip my sweater up in the front. It's still warm, but the ensuing darkness takes away the bite of the sun's heat.

Cast in shadow and with a deep intake of breath, I steel my resolve for what I want to confess to Melanie. "I'm going to return to the US. I don't know how I'm going to do it, but I'm going home, and I'm taking Liam with me."

We stand against the car in companionable silence, listening to the sand's movement. It's constant. With or without any fluctuation of air, the sand continues to move. To mold. To adapt. To change the landscape before us. I need to work out a plan to adapt to the situation I find myself in. Trapped in a country, in a life I no longer want to be a part of, I need to continue to fight and to move forward but with the subtlety of the sand. And quickly— before I'm trapped and suffocated by it.

But, first, I have to say goodbye to Sarah. I must break the cord that holds me in this country. Once I do that, I can work out how to escape. Not to move on ... never to move on. I don't know if I could fully move on from my experiences, my life. But to be free from it, to tackle it and deal with it in a different way. This is what I want, what I need.

I reach into the bag that's been lying half-forgotten at my feet and pull out the reason for our foray into the desert. It's a small wooden jewelry box. Handmade in Jordan, it's simple in design with its rectangular shape. There is no clasp to lock it, just a small hinge to connect the body of the box to the lid. What's special about this box is the mosaic-like pattern depicting a flower from the region on its lid. A desert rose. Such a simplistic name for a plant that survives the heat and desert. I marvel at the thought of anything surviving in this barren wasteland.

But it's time to move on.

It's time to harness all the hurt, anguish, and guilt and shape it into something else. For me to move forward and continue moving forward, I need to do something to symbolize Sarah. To allow me to say goodbye for now. My resolve to find her needs to be put on hold while I work out a way to free myself from the shackles of this country and my disastrous marriage.

I gather yet another handful of sand, but instead of letting the breeze take it, I pour it into the jewelry box as I whisper my promise to my absent daughter. "In this place, at this time, I say goodbye. I don't want to, and it's not fair. But life's not fair, and I need to concentrate on tomorrow and keep living. I hope and pray that wherever you are, Sarah, you are well. I will keep searching. I'll never give up. Never."

With a click, the lid to the box holding the desert sand is secured. I run my fingers over the uneven surface of the mosaic design. Sarah loved the desert roses. She couldn't believe such a beautiful thing could grow so easily and flourish in a place devoid of water and dirt. I hope I've captured a part of her spirit and soul with the sand in the box.

I press my lips to the rough wood surface and gaze up into the night sky. The stars are becoming visible, and a surreal feeling overcomes me as I watch them appear in the silence of the desert.

"Do you think Sarah's alive? Do you think she can see the stars from where she is?" My words are whispered into the night.

"Maybe?" Melanie answers on a sigh as she, too, stares into the night sky. "I hope so."

I watch my friend leaning back against the car as a small tear trickles down the side of her face. None of this has been easy … for anyone. The events are a stark reminder that life-changing events can happen to anyone at a moment's notice. They are indiscriminate and uncaring. Melanie's friendship over the past weeks has been unfailing. Without her steadfast support and guiding voice, I don't think I could have survived the duplicitous game we were forced to play with our friends, family, and the media. The white lies and half-truths, all in an attempt to try to save Sarah, to get her home. All worthless and seemingly designed to protect everyone, except us and Sarah.

I look down to the jewelry box held tightly in my hands and close my eyes. I move the box up to my chest, letting it rest beside my ravaged heart. Somehow, throughout this ordeal, it has continued to beat. I gather strength from this and offer up a prayer to anyone who will listen, praying that Sarah's heart beats as well. I need to believe it does. I'm not sure how I could survive if I found out otherwise.

Darkness has fallen completely when I open my eyes. Even with muted light being provided by the moon and stars, the desert appears limitless. But it's the silence. The silence surrounds us; it envelops us.

I clutch my small part of Sarah with renewed vigor, not wanting to let her go. I need to get out of this place before the silence consumes me.

29

My mind has cleared since saying my goodbyes to Sarah and capturing a tiny part of her spirit in the rose-garnered jewelry box. It's been two long and heartbreaking days, but it was the right decision and has allowed me to redirect my emotions and focus on my escape. The word *escape* sounds so ridiculous. I'm supposedly living a five-star life. Why would I want to leave? Cast aside the facts that my ten-year-old daughter has been abducted and possibly sold into child sex slavery, my twelve-year-old son is becoming a recluse, my husband is an adulterer, and I live in a country whose laws and recent inaction condones all of this, I have minimal rights. My country's hands are tied, and they can't help me. Me—an American citizen, wife, and mother. The world is crazy if it thinks it can influence anything to help me and my son go home without dire consequences. I'm sure it'll all sort itself out with the luxury of time, but time is slowly killing me.

I'm a lost soul going through the motions of living. It's gradually strangling me, choking the life out of me. I don't know whether going back to the US by myself would be a better option. Every time I think it would, I think of Liam. I can't leave him here.

I've been racking my mind for a way that both of us could leave. Staying here isn't much of a life, but we'd at least be together. If I could, I would pack us both up and just go. But I can't run the risk of attempting to leave the country with the threat of arrest or deportation hanging over my head. I can't afford the black smear to be put next to my name.

Working through all the options available doesn't leave any viable solutions. Kevin has made it abundantly clear that he doesn't want to try to make our marriage work. He's moved on, and although I think his words and actions will one day find him remorseful and regretful ... he doesn't feel that now. But, if I'm honest with myself, too much has been said and done between us to recover from it.

I've considered some of the illegal options of getting us out of the country. By small boat or aircraft, smuggled into another country, if not all the way home. But, by paying to use these people smuggling services, I'd be condoning the illegal activities that are part of how my daughter was taken from us in the first place. It'd be our luck that, instead of getting out and getting home, the dollar signs over our heads due to our nationality and skin color would have us redirected into something more ominous and deadlier. Something we didn't pay for. Something to trap us. I've had friends who considered smuggling their children back to the US, but the thought of them being alone and drugged for parts of the journey was a deal-breaker. As it is for me.

One thing might work. I have an appointment today with the US Embassy. It's a long shot, but I'm going to ask if I qualify for help in leaving the country with Liam under extenuating circumstances. I'm expecting them to say no, but there's no harm in asking. At least they'll be aware of my situation and of the change in my circumstances. They'll hopefully be more sympathetic to my plight than the Dubai family courts would be.

The car door slams and traps me inside with the sweltering heat. I make no effort to turn the ignition on to allow the cool air from the air-con to flow. Resting my head on the steering wheel, I watch the droplets of my tears hit and cool on the hard vinyl before making their way down to fall onto my thighs.

The embassy was a bust. They can't help me if Kevin goes through the local courts because the local law will have jurisdiction, and they won't use their political clout to get me past the security at immigration. Of course, if we were on US soil, it would be different. Divorce, custody laws, and the way they're handled are not the same. If I were home, I wouldn't need the embassy. I wouldn't be dealing with this situation. But here, there's not a level playing field. The embassy doesn't have any authority, and their hands are tied. Their sympathies and wishes are of no help to me.

If Kevin wants to place a travel ban on Liam's passport, that's his prerogative. There's nothing I can do about it, except appeal it in the courts. I suppose what it comes down to is where we file for divorce. If we file in the US, it entitles me to half of our assets. If we file in the UAE, I'm entitled to only what I own, which isn't much, since most of our assets are held in Kevin's name and I haven't worked in over a decade.

If the divorce is processed through the local legal system, as the biological mother, I'll be classified as only Liam's custodian, not his guardian. It means I'll only be allowed to do the day-to-day upkeep and caring for him. In fact, under the UAE federal law, I might not even be appointed Liam's custodian because he's over the age of eleven, meaning Kevin has the law completely on his side if he wants sole custody of Liam. I can fight it in court, requesting to look after Liam until he completes school, but Kevin can work around this. He can claim full custody of his only male child if he believes Liam will become too soft in nature by staying with me. That he shouldn't be with me if he's to grow into a responsible man. That's all he has to say to the judge to take my son away from me.

My earlier thoughts about fleeing the country were put to rest after the warnings I received from the embassy staff. To take a child out of the country without the other parent's consent is considered child abduction. How ironic is that? Having just lost one child, I don't plan on losing another.

The only avenue I can see open to me is to report Kevin's infidelity. If I can prove him guilty of adultery in a local court of law, he will be arrested and probably spend time in prison before being deported home. As much as the thought of Kevin sitting in a jail cell brings me joy, it's not something I'm prepared to do for the sanctity of our ongoing relationship as parents to our child. Children. It's just not worth it. Plus, the burden of proof for obtaining a conviction for adultery is high, and my one photo isn't going to be enough.

My head nearly exploded after going through all this with the embassy staff. All the dos and don'ts. The political fallout from helping me isn't a risk they're willing to take. This could change, but until then, I'm stuck. Who knew living in a foreign country as an expat could get so difficult and messy? Who would expect you'd need to fight for your rights to be a wife or mother?

I turn the key in the ignition and wait for the relief from the cool air blowing through the vents. I'm a mess. The heat and humidity have glued my clothes to my body, using my sweat as the binding agent. The reflection in the mirror of a splotchy face marred by blackened streaks has me groaning. I need to make myself presentable, as I have one more stop to make.

It's futile and probably suicidal, but I need to know. In a last-ditch effort, I've decided to seek advice from someone who definitely won't be happy to see me and who probably won't help me—Lieutenant Ahmed, Dubai Police.

30

———

"Mrs. Johnson, what is so important that one of the officers can't help?" Lieutenant Ahmed asks with an air of irritation as I'm led into his office.

It's nice, very spacious. Paintings of local dignitaries adorn the walls. The faces of the two sheikhs silently berate me for the intrusion through their oil paint strokes.

"*A-salaamu aleikom, Mulazim.*" I offer the formal greeting and stand in front of the closed door, awaiting his reply.

There's a moment of silence as we regard each other.

"*Wa aleikoma-salaam.* Please, Mrs. Johnson, please take a seat, *ta-fadl.*" He stands and indicates the chairs positioned around a coffee table under the large glass windows. "Tea?"

I'm not a fan of the Arab tea, but I nod in acceptance of his offer. From a side table, he places two small cups on a tray with the teapot and walks over to where I'm sitting. The tray thuds gently as it's placed on the coffee table. Lieutenant Ahmed adjusts the skirts of his *thobe* before he sits across from me.

Unsure of the protocol for whom should pour the tea, I take the initiative and do it myself. Steam rises as the amber liquid fills the cups. The heat from it is a warm welcome to my chilled body. Unlike the conversation I'm about to start, the tea is sweet.

"I want to return to the US, Lieutenant," I start.

His eyebrows rise slightly as he takes a sip of his tea before placing the cup down.

I look away and focus on a palm tree outside the window as I continue, trying to conceal the emotions from my voice. "Since the investigation into Sarah's abduction is … closed, there's not much else we can do from here. I think I can gain better support from my government if I'm back in the US. It would also mean I can use other avenues to search for her myself that won't cause waves with your government."

"Good. This is good, Mrs. Johnson. Thank you for letting me know. When do you leave?" He steeples his fingers under his chin as he watches me.

If it were only that simple. If only I could just pack up and leave.

Despite his words of encouragement, I can't work out if the lieutenant thinks my leaving is good or not. Not that it should affect him in any way.

My hands have started to shake, and some of my tea spills onto my skirt, soaking in to leave a damp stain. I take a deep breath and uneasily set the cup on the table before another mishap can occur.

"My husband and I are getting a divorce, and I want to take Liam back to the US. Kevin … doesn't agree with my plan, and he's put a travel ban for Liam in place." There's a quiver in my voice, and the words lack the strength I wanted them to have. Instead of being firm and assertive, I can feel my resolve crumbling as doubt for my reasons to be here begins to creep in.

Lieutenant Ahmed grunts in understanding. He picks up his teacup and looks directly into my eyes before taking a drink. It's unnerving, and I break eye contact and look away in embarrassment.

"I understand losing a daughter would put strain on a relationship, but it is not my job to offer you marital advice. You should resolve your differences and be a better wife or take it to the courts to settle," he deadpans.

My shattered nerves dissipate at his words for me to be a better wife. As if everything could be resolved if I were a better wife. If I had done my wifely duties without question or complaint. Sometimes, I pity the women born into this culture. But I suppose, if you grow up thinking this is what life is, then you don't know any better.

My jaw clenches, and I narrow my eyes while looking at him. "It's more complex than that, *Lieutenant.*" I say his rank with emphasis, showing my disdain for him and his words. As I keep my voice low, the words come out with an edge to them, flowing over my tongue with venom. "It's not just about Sarah. My husband's been having an affair, and he doesn't want to reconcile. He wants a divorce so he's free to move on with his mistress. I refuse to stay here and be the third wheel just so Liam can finish school. He can finish school at home, in the US."

My face turns numb as I realize what I just admitted to the lieutenant. That my husband has committed adultery.

Lieutenant Ahmed's expression, however, does not change. He's looking at me with a stern expression. The cup in his hand has stilled in front of him, and he takes no action to move it.

"Do you have proof of this?" His tone gives away nothing.

I close my eyes.

What have I done?

Why can't some things get lost in translation?

"Yes, I do. I have—" I whisper, but he cuts me off before I can tell him I have a photo and the names of a few of his office employees who would be willing to make a statement. That Kevin's confessed his sins, albeit not in writing or recorded on any device, but a person's word has to count for something.

"Do you want to press charges? This is something we take very seriously in the UAE. Not like your American laws." His voice sounds gruff through the accented words. I feel as though I'm being simultaneously judged and condemned by them.

I wipe away a stray tear and return my hand to grip the other one in my lap. "I know, I know. I don't want to officially report him. That's not why I came here. I was just hoping …" The words refuse to come out, as I'm having trouble breathing. It all comes down to this single point. The point where I am hoping to beg a favor. Hoping an Emirati police officer will bend the rules for an American woman and her child. Hoping something good can come out of all the bad.

"Hoping what, Mrs. Johnson?" I hear the irritation in his voice. It's as though he's guessed what I want.

I look down at my hands as I wring them in my lap. Uneven nails, some with jagged edges from where they've broken or torn, lacking any color or polish.

"I just want to take my son and go home," I whisper to my hands, not wanting to look up. "But I can't because there's a travel ban in place."

"Mrs. Johnson, I am not sure what you are trying to say. This is the United Arab Emirates. The law is the law. If you try to leave, you will be arrested. That is the law." His words are said matter-of-fact and without feeling, as though he were reading out the charges laid against me to a judge.

I blink back the tears and clench my hands into fists once again. My words, when they come out, are so soft that a pin hitting the brightly colored rug could make more noise. "I know. I want to leave, but if we try, my son will lose another family member. It's just not right."

After a minute's silence, keeping my eyes downcast, I stand and leave the room.

31

After leaving the lieutenant's office, I drove home under a black cloud.

My options are limited, and the trade-off for getting what I want isn't really worth it.

At the moment, my cup is completely empty, and I'm pulling my hair out, trying to work out how to fill it back up. I want to be optimistic, but it's just not looking good.

I growl, placing my elbows on the kitchen table so that my hands can massage my temples. I've been searching the internet for an hour, trying to find an alternative solution. Google doesn't have any suggestions, and I'm out of ideas.

I push the laptop away in disgust and pull the papers sitting off to the side toward me. I've listed all our assets both in Dubai and back at home in the US, trying to work out what I'll be able to access easily enough and what will help me set up a new life. Trying to second-guess what Kevin will part with and what's a reasonable request. I'm not going to file for divorce in this country where I'm entitled to nothing. I'll find a lawyer back home who'll take into consideration my worth to the marriage and the progression and fast-tracking of Kevin's career.

My concentration is shattered as the doorbell rings. I consider not answering it. Anika's not here to do it for me, as I sent her out, not wanting her around while I was reviewing the personal documents. The bell rings twice more, and I stand, pushing away from the table. Whoever it is, is impatient.

I open the front door and peer out to the gate. There's a courier standing in the driveway, his motorcycle parked adjacent to him on the side of the road. He's about to press the external doorbell again when he looks up and sees me standing in the villa's entranceway.

"Mrs. Johnson?" he calls after reading off my name from his clipboard.

"Yes," I respond, disinterested.

Kevin occasionally gets work delivered home. We normally sign for it and leave it on the desk in the office. To my knowledge, he hasn't had anything delivered over the past few weeks. Not that it matters since he hasn't been around all that much. I clench my fists when I realize why that is and where his deliveries are being sent to now.

"Madam, I have something for you. I will need you to sign for it," he says, holding a clipboard in one hand, tapping his pen to it with his other.

"Okay," I say slowly, dragging the word out.

I'm perplexed, as I'm not expecting a delivery. If it's correspondence from the embassy, they would have told me about it when I was there earlier today. It would make more sense if it were from a media outlet. I purse my lips, thinking about the hot water I could get in for accepting something from the media. My eyebrows furrow as I contemplate if it's court papers.

Would Kevin have already filed for divorce or something else?

I unlock the gate to take the clipboard from the courier and sign the paperwork. He smiles and hands over a letter-sized envelope addressed to me, not Kevin.

"Thank you," I say, adding a slight smile.

I wonder if I can get away with burning the papers inside on my gas stovetop. If I don't acknowledge them and destroy them before I read them, then they're not real. Are they?

The courier has already put away the paperwork and has stepped astride the seat of the bike when he turns back to me. "You're welcome, madam. *Mulazim* Ahmed sends his regards."

I freeze at his words.

Lieutenant Ahmed?

The envelope is firmly clutched between my fingers as I walk back to the kitchen, opening the envelope as I go. Inside is the white-and-gold lettering of the Emirates Airlines. My hands shake as I lift it and pull it open, ripping the little sticker holding it closed in the process. As I scan the paperwork, it's as though the weight of the world has left my shoulders. This is too good to be true, but I don't know what it means.

I send a quick text message to Melanie, saying I need to see her immediately. What I have to say can't be said over the phone, running the risk of it being overheard by whoever's listening. I scroll through my phone contacts, looking for the number I have for Taylor, and hit the call button. This morning, at the embassy, I overheard she was in the country on official FBI business. I only hope it's true.

Taylor answers on the first ring.

"I need your help," I say into the phone with urgency mixed with fear, not bothering with any pleasantries or identifying who I am.

"Okay," she replies, instantly on alert. "I'll be right there."

32

———

Taylor has just left the villa when Melanie arrives. I'm full of nervous energy, like I'm strung out from too much caffeine.

Melanie gives me a strange look as I greet her, half-hidden behind the front door. As she steps through, I throw one last furtive look up the street. I don't know what I'm looking for, but whatever it is, it isn't there. Hopefully.

"What's going on, Jen?" Melanie asks, brows pinched and confusion lacing her voice as she follows my gaze up the street. Her eyes study mine for a minute before she gasps, face turning ashen. A hand comes up to cover her open mouth as she whispers, "Oh no. Is it Sarah?"

With my back against the front door, I frantically shake my head. Tears roll down my cheeks. I need to speak, to assuage her fear, but the jitters make me irrational.

"No," I manage to croak out, taking her hands in mine and jumping up and down.

She cocks an eyebrow and tilts her head to the side, staring at me as though I'm crazy. A giggle erupts from me, which has her eyebrow arching higher. Maybe I *am* crazy. It would be understandable, considering what I've been through.

"I'm going home. Tonight … I think," I say and pull her after me toward the kitchen. I grab the white-and-gold envelope from the table and thrust it into her hands. "Look."

"Okay," she says slowly, pulling the tickets and itinerary out of the envelope. "First class, nice. Hang on, these are for tonight?" she says, bringing her eyes back up to mine in confusion. "What do you mean, *I think*? What's going on?"

I sit and quickly recount the highlights of my day and how, up until thirty minutes ago, my options were limited. How my options might still be limited. That, if I go through with this and try to use these tickets for Liam and me to return home, I could be arrested and end up in jail on child abduction charges.

She reaches across the table and clasps my hand in hers. "This is it, Jen. You have to do this," she says firmly.

"But what if it's an elaborate trap to arrest me? I don't know for sure where the tickets came from. And the parting words from a courier is hardly anything to gamble my life away for." These are the words I speak out loud to air my fears. I know what I want to do, what I'm going to do, but I need to hear what Melanie has to say in case I am in fact crazy and this is in fact a crazy idea.

"You need to take the chance. You need to believe this is real. Get home, deal with all the crap with Kevin, and start over. Create a new life for you and Liam." Tears shine on her cheeks as she speaks, the small smile a contradiction.

I stand and bring her into my arms as she starts crying in earnest. The past few weeks have been hard on everyone close to us, and the cost of each and every tear shed has been painstakingly high. But, this time, as the tears streak our faces, each droplet comes with the promise of hope.

She steps back, releasing me from the hug, and wipes away the wetness with the back of her hand. Black streaks surround her glistening eyes as she briefly studies me. "Let's get you guys packed. We've got an hour before the Emirates first-class limousine service will be here to take you to the airport."

Adrenaline courses through my body. If I thought I was nervous earlier, I was wrong.

Liam looks across from the back seat and screws up his face in concern before giving a pointed look at my knee. It appears to be shaking, but it's acting as a piston for the furious heel tapping, which is the result of my building anxiety. Closing my eyes, I take in a slow, deep breath to help control my restlessness. I'm on edge, and the sensation is intensifying as it combines with a feeling that I am doing something wrong and that there's a chance I'll be caught.

Emirates first-class check-in has its own private entrance. As we pull up in front, we're greeted by Taylor, who helps us unload our three bags.

"Listen, I've run a check and called in a favor with an FBI tech. As far as we can see, the tickets are legitimate," she says softly, positioning her body so as not to be overheard.

I indicate to Liam to stay with the bags as Taylor and I move a few feet away for added privacy. I'm hoping she'll be able to tell me who purchased the tickets and whether or not there's a ban in place for Liam.

"They were purchased this afternoon, and whoever bought them had enough clout to get you last-minute seats and keep their identity secret." She half turns to look at Liam. As she faces me again, her eyes flash with concern when she continues. "I couldn't tell if the travel ban on Liam has been lifted though. To find out for sure, it would've raised more red flags than anything else, so I thought it best to leave it and hope it's been taken care of."

"I understand," I say.

Not knowing if the ban is in place is a concern, but if what she's saying regarding the ticket sale is true, then maybe Lieutenant Ahmed is behind it all. He warned me I'd be arrested if I attempted to fly without Kevin's approval, so why give me tickets to return home if I was only going to be taken into custody? None of it makes sense.

I'm about to join Liam and head inside when Taylor reaches out and grabs my arm to stop me.

"I've cleared it with my superiors back in Washington to come with you and help you get through the process. I'll run interference if need be. What we're doing might be against UAE law, but it's in that gray area that could fall either way. I'm here mainly to support you and your son and to assist as I'm best able. But even though my superiors are aware of what's going on, I'm not here in an official capacity. I can flash my badge and query something, but if it becomes official, I'm going to have to step away. I want to help but am only able to assist up to a certain point. Our aim is to get you into international airspace. After that, the US government can help more."

My vision becomes blurry, and I blink away the mist. I'm happy, knowing I'm not going to have to go through this alone. It might all be for nothing, but with every step I've taken since signing for those tickets, it feels as though I'm headed in the right direction.

Taylor picks up a small blue duffel bag and shrugs it over a shoulder. "Let's go check in," she says, smiling brightly and walking over to join Liam.

We head to the Emirates counter. Handing over our passports and tickets, I hold my breath, waiting for any indication that there'll be an issue, but there is none. Our bags are tagged and sent off on the conveyer belt, and I watch them disappear through the small door to the rear.

Three bags—that's all Liam and I packed. Three bags closer to leaving.

Boarding passes were our first hurdle. Although relieved security wasn't called and I wasn't dragged away somewhere, it's not over. We still need to go through immigration. Their computers will scan the visa pages in our passports and unveil the truth.

The knots in my stomach are twisting so hard, I think I'm going to be sick. It takes a concerted effort to stand in the immigration line. The white marbled tiles and overly high ceilings showcase the spaciousness of this hidden oasis. The only downfall is there are only two exits— behind me and in front of me, past the immigration officers. With this side of the terminal only catering to business and first-class ticket holders, the three immigration desks open are more than enough to get everyone through quickly. It gives me no time for second thoughts.

I watch furtively as an official wearing his starched white *thobe* returns the stamped passport of the person in front. He raises his hand, and with a slow flick, he calls Liam and me forward. As we step up to his workstation, Taylor gives me a reassuring nod from where she stands in the adjacent line.

I hand over our boarding passes and passports and offer up a silent prayer.

Time moves slowly as he flicks through the pages of my passport, looking at my residency visa, repeating the process with Liam's. He looks up to verify that we're the people in the photos and that the names match those on the boarding passes. He then scans the passport in his machine and checks the corresponding data that has come up on the screen.

I hold my breath. This is the moment of truth.

The adrenaline continues to course through my system, and my flight mechanism kicks in as he holds up one finger to indicate I should wait a second. I grip Liam's hand and look for Taylor, fear tightening my face. She has passed through immigration and is standing a few feet on the other side of the counters, waiting for us. Her hands subtly move up and down, telling me to wait, eyes pleading with me to play it cool. The immigration officer has left his workstation and is standing to the side, talking on his cell phone. It feels like eternity before he wraps up his conversation and returns to the desk.

A bead of sweat trickles from my forehead, and I hastily wipe it away with shaking fingers. The official flicks through the pages of our passports again, taking an interest in the stamps on each page. Finding whatever it is he's looking for, he pauses and opens each passport, so they lie flat in front of him. With his free hand, he lifts a silver device from the side of the table and stamps a page in each one.

He looks up as he bookmarks the pages with the boarding passes before closing them, face showing a passive disinterest as he hands the documents over to me and nods toward the direction of the terminal, indicating I can go. With a smile that probably looks more like a grimace, I slowly take them and walk away to the other side where Taylor waits for us, stepping over that imaginary boundary that separates us from the outside. I quickly look back toward the immigration official to see he has pulled out his phone again, not at all concerned with us.

"*Shukran*," I belatedly say, more of a whisper than a spoken word. I'm too far away for him to hear me, not that my manners or niceties would interest him. My thanks are more of a prayer of gratitude to whoever's been looking out for me today than to the immigration officer anyway.

With unspoken relief, we catch the elevator to the level we need to board the plane. Until we're in the air, we're not home free. Immigration isn't the final obstacle, but it was the deadliest. It'll take time to recover from the mini heart attack I suffered when I thought our plans had been foiled.

PART II

33

———

Clouds roll in, blanketing the pain as the rain falls, and the howling wind masks my silent sobs. Throughout this, I stand motionless. Tears camouflaged by the warm rain as I think how things could've been so different. The churning ocean in front of me is a stark contrast to the desert sand.

It's been ten years since Sarah disappeared. Ten years since devastation hit my family and its aftershocks sent us to ruin. As I have every year since her disappearance, I say a quick prayer and hope it finds her.

With a deep breath, I take a final look at the turbulent water before returning to where Liam waits for me. At times like these—especially at times like these—I think back to our escape, which is the way I see leaving Dubai. Our departure was nothing short of fantastical. Thinking about it and the aftermath of the last ten years brings a sad smile to my face.

We left Dubai under a dark cloud with no promises of a better future. No promises that we could move beyond the past or that mistakes would or could be forgiven. We snuck away, and it was only pure luck that I didn't end up in a jail cell. Luck and the conscience of a certain police lieutenant. We assume it was Lieutenant Ahmed, but it was never entirely proven he was behind the tickets or the lifting of Liam's travel ban. Honestly, I've never wanted to raise any red flags that could get us all in trouble by trying to find out. Over the years, I've often speculated why this Emirati officer went out on a limb to help, but I only ever came up with two possible scenarios: he either felt guilty for the direction and conclusion of the investigation and its subsequent impact on my family, or he simply wanted us out of the country before we could bring more unwanted media attention on him and his department. Either way, if it was him, I'll be forever grateful.

I'm glad we took the chance and left when we did. I couldn't have continued living in Dubai. The wonder of the city and the glitter of the expat life we'd had was lost the day Sarah was taken. The effect it had on our lives was tumultuous enough, but the secrets it unearthed ... shattering. Kevin would never have let us leave until the divorce and custody were finalized. It's his controlling nature, but I'm probably the first to admit that neither of us was thinking clearly enough to walk through any form of rational decision-making. The impact of losing Sarah and being surrounded by reminders of her on a daily basis was just too much.

We failed her.

Failed her by trusting the system.

We put our faith in the people whose job it was to find her and bring her back to us.

They failed us.

The system's betrayal, coupled with Kevin's infidelity, scarred me deeply. It shattered my soul. Brick by brick, my life was dismantled, and it's taken years to rebuild it from the base up. It'll never be the same, and there will always be some bricks unaccounted for. Gaps in the wall. Gaps in my heart, in my ... soul.

When Liam and I returned, I had lawyers take action to ensure Kevin couldn't follow through with any of his threats. Over time, he's calmed down and accepted things.

He's come to deal with the grief over our loss. And, as much as I wished he were able to do that with me by his side, to walk that road with us as a family, at least he has finally stepped out of the haze of anger that enveloped him for such a long time.

After all the bluster and threats, the divorce and custody of Liam ended up being finalized, uncontested. We moved to Annapolis, which was close enough to both Kevin's and my family if we needed them but far enough away to give us space to do our own thing. Life settled into place with routines set up to heal the remnants of my broken family. Liam received counseling, as did I. Sometimes, we had sessions together, which was eye-opening. I watched my son discuss his self-loathing as he blamed himself for Sarah's disappearance and the subsequent chain of events and how all of his emotions had been festering dark thoughts. I'd never have forgiven myself if anything had manifested from them. This, in itself, told me I'd done the right thing by bringing him home because, if I hadn't, I might have lost more than one child.

Liam's computer gaming interests and his thirst for knowledge continued to grow throughout the years. He recently graduated from the Massachusetts Institute of Technology and is now working in a research lab affiliated with the college. I could not be prouder.

The years have been bittersweet for me. The darkness and time taken while wading through to the gray allowed me to reach a point where I wanted to help others. I wanted to help provide a support system for families who had had their worlds ripped to shreds and weren't sure about the steps to take to minimize the casualties. For this reason, I took a job working for a non-governmental organization that dealt with human trafficking, both domestic and international. I became not only one of their staunch advocates, but also one of the managers for World Watch, based in Washington, DC.

It's devastating, every time I'm called to help a family. But helping them connect to counselors, investigators, and lawyers and holding their hands as they file the paperwork with both our and other governments have been the balm for my broken heart. I both sympathize and empathize with them and can relate on a level that only someone who has been through such an ordeal can.

Sarah.

Every year, her abduction makes the news cycle. An unsolved mystery. A cautionary tale. Every year, we receive information on a possible sighting. New information trickles through a variety of sources. Some just want the outstanding reward we have for any substantial leads, and others come from well-placed organizations. But none have panned out, and I'm starting to think they never will. I don't want to think like that, and it definitely contradicts what I'm doing here today on the anniversary of her disappearance.

Sarah is gone, hidden from us in her final resting place, and it still makes my stomach churn. The hows and the whys behind it all are lost to us, just as she is.

Wet sand cakes the soles of my feet as I take the last few steps to join Liam on sturdier ground. He doesn't say anything as he wraps his arms around my shivering body and moves the umbrella to cover us. He and I share an unbreakable bond forged through grief, deceit, and the discovery of inner strength.

After a few silent minutes of reflection, I lift my head to study my son as his gaze rests on the turbulent waves of the Atlantic.

Sarah might be lost, but she's not forgotten.

The rain eases as the sun briefly breaks through the clouds on the horizon, reflecting a choppy pathway on the ocean's face. I often wonder where such a path could lead. Does it hold the answers I seek? The cloud formations change with the winds. They move again to block the sun, and the imaginary pathway holding all my answers disappears. As it recedes into nothing, I say a final prayer for Sarah.

If I could, I would follow the path. One day, I will … and then I'll know.

With my final prayer, I turn to Liam. "Let's go home."

34

———

The doorbell rings, and Liam, for once, jumps out from behind his computer to answer it. I know he's too old to be living at home, but we found out a few years ago that we made good housemates. It was trial and error for him throughout college, but he finally came to the same realization. It warms my heart to have him close. The house is big enough, and with our work and social schedules, neither of us spends that much time under the roof for it to be a problem.

"I've got it, Mom," he yells, rushing to the front door.

I laugh at his eagerness. He's been waiting two days for UPS to deliver a new gaming headset. It's either that or he's expecting his girlfriend. They've been spending a lot of time together over the past few months. I'd be hard-pressed to guess which one would be more responsible for his excitement. It's been great, watching Liam's evolution over the years, and I'm proud to be his mother.

"Mom, it's for you." His voice sounds different, guarded with a hint of warning. The silence that settles over the house with his words is oppressive. It's as though the walls and windows were trying to send me a sign.

With a dark foreboding, I set the dishes I've been drying on the counter and walk to the front door, perplexed. I don't get many visitors, and my plans to catch up with friends for dinner are for later tonight. My forehead crinkles in confusion. If Liam recognized the person at the front door, he would've invited them in.

Suits.

As I turn into the hallway toward the front door, I see suits. The lack of serene expressions and Bibles has me guessing government representatives rather than proselytizing evangelists. The crisp, dark material of the suits is offset with a flash of muted color dangling from their necks, individual touches to what otherwise looks to be the governmental uniform.

There are two of them, standing tall, almost military-like. I reach the door, stand next to Liam, and peer over their shoulders, out into the street, to see a dark sedan with tinted windows. They must be FBI.

"Mrs. Johnson?" the balding one on the right asks.

"Yes. Can I help you?" My voice wavers slightly.

After all these years and the number of government staff and officials I've dealt with, my anxiety shouldn't be an issue, but it's different when they're at the front door. Scenarios for why they're here on a Saturday morning rush through my mind. I don't have any outstanding work cases open that would require FBI interaction. I haven't been dealing with anyone disreputable through work or my own ongoing inquiries.

"Mrs. Johnson, I'm Special Agent Carter, and this is Special Agent Brody." He holds up his identification, confirming he's FBI, and nods his head toward his companion, who has done the same. "If it's not too much trouble, we'd like to have a word with you. Can we come inside, please?"

I shake my head in confusion before realizing my mistake. "What's this about?" I ask cautiously, running my palms up and down my legs.

After a moment of silence that can't be more than three seconds but feels like a year, he answers without emotion. "I think we should come inside."

I quietly lead them into the front sitting room, walking on autopilot as my mind races. The only reason they'd be here, acting so formal, is if it had something to do with Sarah. But if that were the case, Taylor should be here, given her past involvement with the case and our ongoing friendship.

Or is it because of our friendship that she's not here?

My head starts to throb, and the pounding behind my eyes causes the left to twitch involuntarily.

There's a moment of awkwardness as we stand silently, looking at each other, before they sit and expectantly look at Liam and me. Liam has followed us into the room but leans against the wall beside my chair as I hesitantly sit.

I look anxiously at Agent Brody as he clears his throat.

"Mrs. Johnson, we're here chasing down some leads regarding your daughter, Sarah."

I gasp and throw a hand up to cover my mouth. The throbbing behind my eyes intensifies, and my heart skips a beat before increasing its pace. I'm vaguely aware that Liam's kicked off from the wall, and he is now sitting on the armchair beside me, firmly clutching my free hand in both of his.

"Sarah …" I whisper. The word barely makes it past my lips.

We've had leads before but none originating from a government source or any deemed viable enough for government involvement. Their being here means there's some validity to whatever these leads are.

"Yes, that's correct," Agent Carter says, inclining his head a fraction. "Have you received any recent tips regarding possible sightings of your daughter or been in contact with anyone who's seen or spoken to her?"

I look at Agent Carter in confusion. *Why would the FBI be asking me if we had any information on Sarah's whereabouts? They came here because they had some, didn't they? Isn't that what they said?*

His eyes narrow and watch me with an intensity that has me believing he's a human lie detector.

Why do I feel as though I'm on trial?

I pull my shoulders back and take a loud, defensive breath. "No, we haven't. I have no idea what you're talking about. I thought you said *you* had some leads," I say with a small amount of indignation after releasing my breath.

With another frustrated breath, I rake my fingers through my hair before regaining my composure. Convincing myself his demeanor is only part of his job as a special agent and not a slight against me, I bend forward and place my hands on my thighs.

"What's going on?" I ask quietly, inhaling slowly and briefly closing my eyes. I'm suddenly tired, and that reflects in my question.

Agent Carter blinks once and turns toward Agent Brody, somewhat tilting his head.

Taking that as an indication he should speak, Agent Brody clears his throat. "Nothing. We're here doing a routine follow-up. Nothing to get concerned about. You know how it is."

"I thought you were here because you had a lead," I repeat. "We haven't had anything at all remotely worth following up on in over twelve months. Just hoax tips from people hoping to claim the reward. Have you heard something?" Desperation coats my words.

They must know something; otherwise, why make the trek all the way out to see us at home?

"No, no. There's nothing to concern yourself with. As I said, this is just a routine visit." Agent Brody's nostrils flare as he takes a deep breath before averting his eyes.

If I wasn't watching their interactions, I might have missed it. Despair at the realization that I passed the lie detector test and that they actually don't have anything for me infiltrates my lungs with each ragged breath. I gulp, trying to hold the tears at bay. For a few moments—just a few—I started to hope. And hope is always a good thing—until it's gone, until it's proven to be a falsehood. Then, the low after the high is just that much worse.

"We should be going. Thank you for your candor and your time, Mrs. Johnson." Agent Brody stands and brushes off his pants, and Agent Carter follows suit.

I rise slowly, shoulders slumped in defeat, and lead them out much the same way I led them in—trancelike, quietly, and with a million questions racing through my head. My heart still hurts, but it's a different sort of hurt than ten minutes ago. Deeper, intrinsic … desperate.

After their departure, I rest my forehead against the front door, emotions more than likely naked on my face for the world to see. The world isn't present though. It's only Liam and me, as it has been these past long ten years. We often get so caught up in living our lives that we forget the darkness that remained when we lived through this the first time. The emptiness when that section of our souls belonging to Sarah was ripped from our hearts. And it hurts. And each and every time that we get a lead or someone thinks they've seen or heard something, we relive it all over again.

Liam hugs me from behind, resting his head on mine. He doesn't say anything; he doesn't need to. We know. After a moment, he releases me and walks away.

The doorbell chimes just as I sit down in front of the television with a glass of red wine. Not being in the mood for frivolity and laughs, I sent my apologies to my friends for dinner tonight. Cursing under my breath at the rudeness of whoever is at the door for arriving unannounced on a Saturday night and interrupting my self-pity, I place the wine on the coffee table and go to answer it.

Taylor is standing on the other side of the threshold, a grim expression clouding her face. She smiles as I step out and open my arms to pull her into a hug. Holding her shoulders, I pull back to look at her. Her smile doesn't quite reach her eyes.

"Taylor, what a pleasant surprise," I say, letting go of her and heading back inside.

She follows me in, and we make our way to the cozy family room.

"I've just poured myself a glass of wine. Would you like one?"

"That would be great, thanks," she answers and takes off her jacket before sitting.

She's dressed casually, long pants with a pretty pale gray blouse. I've seen her in all modes of dress over the years, and this one isn't her normal off-duty attire. It's telling me she's been doing some sort of informal work today, probably stuck behind a desk in the office.

"You know, you're not the first FBI agent to visit me today. You're much better-looking than the two in monkey suits this morning though," I say, heading into the kitchen to grab a wineglass. I hesitantly wonder if her visit today is related to the one from Special Agents Brody and Carter. Returning to the family room, I hand her the filled glass before sitting again.

I'm not exactly sure what Taylor does now within the FBI. She no longer works hands-on in hostage negotiation or kidnapping cases; she's told me that much. Over the years, she's taken more of a sedentary role with the organization, being given a permanent desk in the Washington, DC, office with staff under her. I'm thankful we've stayed in touch over the years and become close friends.

"I'm not sure about that. Agents Carter and Brody do look good in their suits," she says, letting me know she's aware of their visit. After taking a sip of her wine, she lowers it back down to the table, and her smile disappears. Pursing her lips, she appears to be having trouble with deciding what to say to me. "I'm sorry they turned up on your doorstep this morning. Had I known, I would've stopped them, answered their questions, or if needed, accompanied them." Her somber tone comes out softly and has my hackles rising.

My hands start to shake with the realization that there was more to this morning's visit than I was told. I had a feeling there was. Call it a mother's intuition. My psyche, already raw from the turmoil of emotions let loose this morning, demands questions even though I'm too scared to ask.

"They didn't say much—just that they had some new leads, only to ask if we'd heard anything. After I told them we hadn't had new information in over a year, they left." I take a gulp of the wine, not gaining any pleasure from the fruity taste but hoping an injection of alcohol will calm my fraying nerves.

"There's been a potential sighting," Taylor starts, causing me to snap upright and closely study her. She ticks off things on her fingers as she speaks, her words slow and delivered with measured care. "A woman has come to our attention, and it looks like the timing meets up. Her age matches. There's a likeness between her and the biometrics drawn up of what Sarah would look like as an adult."

"What?" I manage to whisper.

The sightings I've personally followed up on were tips called in to a hotline when stories like Sarah's garnered the media spotlight, causing reporters to dig around and find something to compare them to. Sarah's story is a popular one, compelling as it is complex, pulling the emotional heartstrings as well as drawing out political nuances to match any story.

Over the years, I've had a love-hate relationship with the media. They run our story for nothing more than viewer ratings, but I've always thought the emotional low derived from the retelling and reliving is worth it to keep Sarah alive in the minds of viewers. Someone could have seen or heard something, and having her story in the spotlight reinforces it. I'll never be fully desensitized to the media coverage, but it's something I'm committed to live through.

Most of the time, we don't even investigate. Do-gooders and people wanting to help clog the phone lines, saying they've seen a little girl who resembles Sarah, not even doing the math to work out that she's no longer a child.

Taylor pauses when I put my glass down to wipe the tears from my face.

"I'm glad Brody and Carter weren't authorized to talk to you about it. I wanted to tell you myself. I've been on the phone, talking to sources, and on the computer for most of the day, checking and double-checking to make sure before I came. I'd hate to get your hopes up for nothing." She reaches over and clasps my hand with hers. "But, Jen … this one looks real."

There's a small smile on her face, and I see the hope in her eyes. I think I've forgotten to breathe. Sarah—if it is Sarah—will turn twenty-one next week. She'll be a woman. I blink, wondering, as I always do, what sort of woman she is and what sort of life she's had. In my imagination, she's everything a young woman would want to be.

But the reality could be such a stark difference. If it's true and this is Sarah, the brutality of how her life probably has been is all too real.

Taylor kneels in front of me, and I'm tightly gripping her hands. It's been ten long years since we sat in my Dubai house and hoped we'd find Sarah. Last time, it ended in tears.

Will this time be any different?

"Breathe, Jen. Breathe."

Sarah … she's alive?

I'm hyperventilating.

"Tell me," I force out between breaths.

"There's an oil conference happening in the capital this month. As part of it, we've had attendees arriving from the various oil states. A Saudi, who also happens to be a member of the royal family with ties to the Saudi inner circle, is one of those dignitaries." She pauses to take a breath and gather her thoughts before she continues. "He's brought his family—wife, daughter, son, and his son's family. His son's wife raised some concerns at immigration on entry. She has the CIA and FBI up in arms and confused."

"What do you mean? Wife? Are you talking about Sarah?"

Taylor releases my hand to stand before starting to pace in front of me. With her eyebrows furrowed and pursed lips, I can see she's thinking. This must be an extremely complex issue for her to be acting like this. She halts and swivels in place to scrutinize me, as though determining how she should respond.

"Yes," she says slowly. "We think Salman's wife, Suha, is actually Sarah."

Salman?

Salman's wife?

Suha ... Sarah?

"What does this mean? How can this be? How did Sarah end up with a Saudi family?"

Taylor shrugs and tilts her head to the side. "We have a few working theories, but"—she adds a shake of her head before sitting down across from me once again—"we just don't know. As you can imagine, the Saudis are closing ranks, and the wrong move here could be seen as aggressive and undermine diplomatic relations between Washington and Riyadh."

She pauses as I replay her words in my mind, trying to work out what this all means. I can't wrap my head around Sarah being alive and living with a Saudi family.

"But how?"

"Honestly, Jen, I don't know, but we will find out."

My head falls with a sigh, and I rub my thumb and forefinger over my forehead. When my head lifts again, I meet Taylor's gaze.

"I want to see her."

35

———

Not wanting to wait for the FBI to brief me with their prepared dossier, I spent most of Sunday searching the internet for information and images of the girl-woman who could be my daughter. My searches came up with scant information on the names Taylor provided. Other than official bios for the Saudi royals and links across the kingdom, I found nothing.

As soon as Monday morning hit, I called in favors from every contact I'd made, both in the government and out, since I started working at World Watch. With each call, it was refreshing to realize there was already a significant effort underway, trying to unearth any information. The idea that Suha might be Sarah has all the government agencies combing through their separate databases for information to confirm Suha's heritage. Anything to use as leverage on the Saudi government and the al-Tuhar family to find—or provide—the answers.

The vibration of my cell phone alerts me to a new incoming message. Kevin's been texting me all morning. He's been anxiously waiting for confirmation, one way or the other. The combined excitement and fear has had us talking and texting ever since Taylor left my house. We're both searching for answers. This notification isn't from

Kevin. It's from Taylor, letting me know she emailed me some information. I quickly bring it up on my computer and dial Kevin's number.

"Have you heard anything?" he answers, bypassing any pleasantries. His voice is strained, and I visualize him squinting with a gaze that could stare through a wall, as though it might help him listen.

He's as anxious as I am to hear anything. When I was finally able to contact him early Sunday morning, we were both fearful and hopeful for the news. This time feels different. Something makes me think it's real. Call it intuition. If this *is* Sarah, we'll finally get closure and find out what happened all those years ago.

"No, and I was starting to think everything I was told on Saturday was just a dream. That Suha being Sarah was someone's idea of a bad joke. I've received some files from Taylor, and I'm opening them now."

The text of Taylor's email doesn't contain any pertinent information and is brief and to the point. I click on the file attached, and it opens to show surveillance photos of a young woman.

"Oh my gosh!" My eyebrows rise as my hand covers my mouth. I lean forward, studying the images, sucking my bottom lip between my teeth as my stomach flutters. There's a resemblance.

"What? Jen, what is it?" Kevin's words, spoken softly and with unquestioned urgency, have all the concern I wanted to hear from him ten years ago. It brings me back to the here and now, and I shake my head to align my thoughts.

"She sent some surveillance images of Suha. It's hard to be certain … but she looks like her. Sh-she looks like Sarah." My whispered words carry a spark of hope. I trace the face on the screen with my fingers, and I can't help but smile.

It's her. It really is Sarah!
Oh my God!

"Really? It's her?" he asks hesitantly.

I understand his caution, but if it's not Sarah, this would have to be the cruelest joke.

"Maybe. Hang on; I'll forward the pictures to you."

———

"Can I come in?"

As I'm startled, my eyes dart quickly between the image of the girl on the computer screen and the special agent standing in the doorframe to my office. Hesitantly, I point him into a seat.

"Of course, Special Agent Carter. How can I help you?" I nervously wait for him to speak.

Taylor's email with the photos was leading me to believe Suha was my daughter, but his being here can't be a good sign.

"I wanted to provide you with an update on the investigation." His face is expressionless and has me thinking the worst. "The FBI believes Suha and Sarah are the same person, and as such, the government is in talks with the Saudis to open a diplomatic line of inquiry."

I lean into my chair, back straight, as my mind wanders to the images again. We're one step closer to getting Sarah back. I raise my eyes to look at Special Agent Carter. "What does that mean? By government, do you mean the State Department?"

He scratches his forehead as his brows furrow slightly. "In short, yes. We're trying to get answers and not ruffle any feathers while we do it. It's a very sensitive matter. She's the daughter-in-law of Saudi royalty. If we're wrong …" He trails off, averting his eyes.

I can imagine the political fallout if any accusations made are found unjust. If the State Department is engaging with the Saudis, it means the US government believes Suha is indeed Sarah.

Special Agent Carter clears his throat and straightens his shoulders. Having regained his professional demeanor, he continues in a serious tone. "I know you've been through this before, but I need to remind you not to discuss this with the media, as it could derail everything we're trying to achieve. This also applies to friends and family. Please limit any discussions. I know you and your family are eager to find out if this woman is your daughter, but you need to leave it up to us to investigate. So, no more phone calls."

He gives me a pointed look with his last statement. I swallow quickly, and my cheeks heat.

I'm confident the favors I called in earlier today were with people who know what's at stake and practice the art of discretion. I hope so anyway. The possibility of having Sarah so tantalizingly close makes me anxious and excited, but I realize, more than most, the need to keep things quiet. If a journalist were to get wind of the government-to-government discussions, it would spark immediate media coverage, especially given the links to the Saudi royal family and the implications for the US-Saudi relationship.

"I understand."

Special Agent Carter slaps his hands on his thighs and stands, breaking the somber moment. "Good. That's all I needed to talk to you about. Someone from the department will keep you updated with how the talks go. Just remember, no more phone calls. We'll sort it from here."

I nod in understanding and watch him exit the office.

Not sure of where my emotions lie and needing a moment away from my computer to find my thoughts, I use the sink in the bathroom to splash water on my face. It cools the increasing flush from unanswered questions and gives me a moment to center my thoughts. It's surreal— Sarah, the politics, the intrigue.

When we're reunited, I wonder whether Sarah will recognize the woman staring back at me in the mirror. When she sees the lines around my eyes and mouth, will she understand how I've been able to find a level of happiness, or will she be resentful? On automatic, my fingers tug a stray piece of hair behind my ear, and I pause, noticing the increased peppered strands, so many of which were hard-won over the years.

———

The sound of the Atlantic Ocean crashing onto the shore is the calming melody from my youth that I need right now. I close my eyes and listen to nature's orchestra as a fine layer of salt and sand clings to my skin. Waves crash onto the sand, erupting with the spray the wind blows in my direction. This is representative of the harmonious relationship between the elements, extreme opposites yet complementary. Inhaling the ocean scent, I feel a semblance of peace for the first time in years.

I often think about the ocean off this coastline. It's so vast—home to an extensive network of sea life and vegetation, providing a nurturing home to its inhabitants. Until it doesn't. It can be just as destructive and cruel as it can be nurturing and caring. The sand here though is a giver of life. Seaweed and kelp take root in the shallows, providing nourishment and shelter for various forms of marine life. The sand here works in harmony with Mother Nature to provide—so unlike the cruel and harsh sand of the desert.

As the sun descends into the water, I watch its reflection create a shimmering silver pathway to the horizon, to where the blue of the water meets the blue of the sky. It's therapeutic. On days like today, when I come down to sit, reflect, and say a prayer for Sarah, I used to think, if I were to follow this path, I'd find her. I don't wish upon rainbows, trying to find the treasure at the end of it, because I know it's nothing more than the light refracting through moisture left in the atmosphere after the rain. But I can't help but feel that I'm so close to finding my treasure.

I've been sitting here, thinking, wishing, and dreaming for so long, the tide has receded. The water has withdrawn and exposed more sand in its taunt to me. Daring to take away the hope blossoming in my heart. Daring me to leave. Daring me to break. But I've come a long way, and I will not break. I will not break—partly because I'm already broken, and I've never been able to put the pieces back together. The combined effect of sand, water, and time can smooth out the ragged edges so they're not so sharp. No longer do they cut but instead linger in memory, still broken but unable to slice.

The final glimpse of the sun disappears, taking its warmth with it. With a shiver, I walk back to the car.

When I arrive home, I barely have time to walk through the front door before the phone starts ringing. Reminded of the FBI's warning about potential leaks to the media, I've been screening my calls all day. Seeing the name flashing on my screen, I quickly swipe to answer.

"Taylor, do you have an update?"

"I do. The Saudis have agreed to DNA testing."

My free hand instinctively clasps my chest. Adrenaline courses through my bloodstream, causing my heart rate to spike. With a deep breath and steady exhale, I curb my emotions to respond. "Really? That's great news. How long will the results take?"

"We'll retrieve a sample tonight and have it rushed through the labs and tested against yours and Kevin's, which are already in the database. We should get confirmation one way or another in a few days."

"A few days? I could have my daughter back in a few days?" I sink into the couch, the relief palpable.

There's a pause on the phone.

"If we get confirmation Suha is your daughter, we'll look at setting up a meeting straightaway." Taylor pauses a moment and continues softly. "Jen, I know, in your mind, she's still your little girl, but if this *is* Sarah, you need to remember that she's a legal adult. Despite the situation, she'll need to make her own decisions on whether she stays here or not."

"What do you mean?"

"I don't think you should have any expectations, and I don't think you can pressure her to stay. Suha is married. She has a family and is happy. If it is Sarah, you'll have a chance to build a new relationship with her and her family, but that's all. You can't force anything on her."

My heart plunges as I lose the wind in my sails. "I-I think I'd be happy, just knowing she's alive and well," I whisper into the phone.

It's a lie.

I want so much more. I want to bring her home, to be her family, and to get back all the years we lost. To care for her and protect her. I don't want to share her with another family. I want to save her from them.

I want to be her mother.

Her mother.

Hers.

I want this so much.

But, as much as I hate Taylor's words, I know she's right.

"The Saudis have closed ranks around the family, and we don't really know what's going to happen. Just a few more days, and then we'll know. But ... it looks like the real thing."

"I know," I reply softly.

I know in my heart that this is Sarah. It has to be.

There's another pregnant pause before Taylor continues in a hushed voice, her words freezing me in place. "She ... Suha and Salman have a son. And she's pregnant."

Sarah has a son?

Warmth spreads through my body as a smile curves my lips. If Sarah has a son, it makes me a grandmother. I'm a grandmother.

"And the child? My grandson?" I choke on a sob as the words pass my lips, and I absently swipe away the stray strands of hair stuck to the wetness on my face.

"Iskander, and he's almost two."

Iskander. The Arabic name for Alexander. A strong boy's name, both in Arabic and English.

I lick my lips and close my eyes, imagining a rambunctious toddler with soft blond curls, running around, causing mischief.

"Iskander," I repeat.

With that one word, that one thought, my whole focus tilts. My wants and my needs change in an instant. Taylor's right; if Suha is my daughter and she's happy with her family and life, I can't make demands. But I do want to foster a relationship. I want that more than anything.

"How long after the DNA is confirmed can we meet them?"

36

———

I exit my car and hand the keys to the valet. We're meeting the Saudis later today and, hopefully, Sarah. But, first, I'm going to see Kevin and let him read the file the FBI dropped off yesterday. Things have been weird between us recently. The feelings of betrayal and guilt I had over my failed marriage are long gone. In its place is a calm camaraderie, reminiscent of the time before we had kids. As strange as this new dynamic is for us, today is about Sarah and her return.

The FBI hasn't been able to meet with Kevin in person, partly because he was out of state. It's not a surprise. He still travels so much for work. I suppose we were just lucky that he was only out of the state and not the country.

My smile freezes when I see him standing in the hotel reception area with Jacquie. I grind my teeth at the audacity of her being here on a day meant for my family. Over the years, I've gotten good at avoiding her. I wish I could avoid her today.

Kevin walks over and embraces me. My body instinctively molds against his, as it's been programmed to do, as his arms hold me tight. The familiar warmth and smell soothe me and immediately alleviate my feelings of anxiety. Regardless of what's been said or happened in the past, this man is my first love and the father of my children. Years apart have given me the clarity to see the mistakes we both made, and for the sake of Liam—and, now, Sarah—I've made my peace with them.

As Kevin steps away from me, Jacquie looks on, expressionless. Time might have passed, but the wounds left by her betrayal have yet to heal. If I'm being honest, I haven't really found peace with their infidelity. Part of me acknowledged this years ago as something I needed to accept for what it was and move on. I've tried.

"It's good to see you, Jen. You're looking well."

"Thanks. So are you."

He does look well, but that doesn't really come as a surprise to me. Kevin was always one to take care of himself.

"Let's take a seat, and you can tell me what's going on. The voicemail I received from the FBI after our flight didn't make much sense." Kevin gestures toward a sitting area that offers a bit more privacy.

As we head in that direction, he takes the time to stop one of the hotel staff and ask for coffee to be brought to the table. My body sinks into the plush lounge as Kevin and Jacquie take the opposite seats. She runs her hands down her dress, ensuring it's sitting just right, and crosses her legs so the base of her stilettos are facing me. The stitching and signature red sole identify them as Louboutins. Memories of my life in Dubai among the expat wives and their thirst for everything designer flood back. The shoes are meant to represent something, but other than a huge extravagance, they mean nothing to me now.

"So, what's the latest? Have the Saudis acknowledged that Suha is Sarah?" His face scrunches up as he says her name, *Suu-har*, but it doesn't mask the anxiety coming off him.

I can relate to the fear on his face. Like me, he thought the worst. He thought Sarah had been sold into slavery.

"No, they haven't because it would open them to all sorts of kidnapping and conspiracy charges. But it *is* Sarah. She's apparently been in Saudi Arabia all this time, living with a family," I say gently, removing the envelope containing photos out of my bag and placing them on the table. I swallow, and I shoot a quick look at Jacquie as I think of the images he has yet to see.

Kevin tilts his head to one side, picking up on my nervousness. The envelope sits on the table between us, untouched. "Are you sure? Are you sure it's her?"

I read the confusion on his face. He probably thinks I'm upset because this girl isn't our daughter. Why should I be nervous if I truly believe she is Sarah?

"It's her. The DNA test confirms it. It's her, Kevin." I can't prevent the tears from falling. I promised myself I wouldn't cry again, but I can't help it. After all this time, finding Sarah is unbelievable.

"Sarah's alive?" Kevin's words are spoken softly, reverently, and his eyes blink rapidly.

His hand reaches out to cover Jacquie's, and I look away as he gains this support and reassurance from her.

"Yes. She's alive. Take a look," I prompt, pushing the envelope toward him, breaking the moment.

"When does she get here?" Jacquie asks, looking around as if expecting Sarah to join us in the foyer, her eyes flicking between the exits. "And how could they verify her identity so quickly? These cases normally take a lot longer to process. Who's the legal representative?"

I ignore her and concentrate on Kevin as he takes the photographs from the envelope. His hands start to shake as he looks at the first image of Sarah. She's dressed in an intricate summer dress with gold sandals, and the image captured has her laughing at someone out of shot. She looks carefree and happy. Kevin's tears contrast with the smile as he looks at the image with wonder.

This is undoubtedly our Sarah. And Kevin agrees.

He raises his head, looks at me over the photo, and nods. He clears his throat and whispers her name. "Sarah."

I'm overcome with emotion as I nod back in confirmation. My response also comes out as a whisper as I choke back the sobs. "Yes, Kevin, it's our daughter."

"Oh my God." Kevin puts down the photos and buries his face in his hands. His shoulders shake as tears flow freely.

Jacquie wraps her arms around him and rocks with him. I avert my eyes to avoid intruding on their moment. Minutes pass until Kevin brings his emotions under enough control to look through the remainder of the photos.

As he scans the remaining photos, I voice the questions I have over the identity of the men who have been photographed with Sarah. "Kevin, do you recognize any of the men with Sarah? I know it's a long shot … but I can't shake the feeling that I've seen them somewhere before. I don't know if it's just wishful thinking or an overactive imagination. The FBI asked me if I recognized them, but I wasn't sure. Do you?"

Kevin reviews the photos one at a time. When he reaches the one with the older gentleman, Jacquie's intake of breath has me looking at her, not Kevin. She meets my eyes and quickly looks away. In that moment, I remember what my mind has been trying to recall ever since the FBI showed me these images. It's not Kevin who knows the people photographed. It's Jacquie.

"No! Tell me it's not true, Jacquie." My voice trembles, and my hands are shaking.

"What's not true?" Kevin asks, looking up from the photos.

I reach across and snatch the last photo from his hands. The one with the older Saudi, who the FBI told me was Nayef al-Tuhar, second cousin to the Saudi king.

"This," I say, waving the photo in front of them. "Jacquie, tell him."

"I-I ..." she stutters, which is probably a first for her, and it indicates she's shaken.

But, with her hesitation, I know my answer.

"You knew?" I ask incredulously.

"No! I didn't know. I had no idea who had taken her. If I had known, I would've said something when she was taken," she says, pulling her shoulders back, not quite meeting my eyes.

My mind is working overtime as I carefully take in her words.

"You didn't know ... but you worked it out, didn't you? You had an idea of where she might've been taken?" I say slowly and deliberately. I place my hand on the table and lean forward.

Jacquie bites her lip and looks away but not before I read the guilt in her glistening eyes.

"Answer the question, Jacquie," Kevin demands. He drops the photos on the table as he swivels in his seat to face her, placing space between the two of them.

At his harsh words, she looks up at him.

"I-I ..." she stutters again before taking a deep breath and regaining some of her composure. "I had my suspicions. But not when she was taken. It wasn't until years after Sarah's disappearance that I thought I heard or saw something ... I-I didn't know for sure. It was just a suspicion."

A whimper escapes me as Kevin continues the interrogation. "Why didn't you say something?"

She turns away slightly, defensively folding her arms across her chest. "What should I have said? What would I have said? This?" She takes the photo with the older man in the frame and points to him. "This is Nayef al-Tuhar. He was a client of mine. His affairs are covered by attorney-client privilege ..."

Kevin grabs her arms and starts shaking. "Bullshit. You could've said something." His action and words draw the attention of the hotel employees.

I tune the two of them out as I realize what was nagging me about that photo. It's like someone has thrown a bucket of ice water over me. I sit up straighter in my seat, my thoughts in overdrive. Images shuffle through my mind, like someone flicking the pages of a flip book in reverse. Suddenly, I understand. It all makes sense. Jacquie was on our return flight that summer from the US to Dubai. The kids and I saw her when she was boarding with the other first-class travelers. Sarah saw her first and went over to say hello.

Jacquie was traveling with clients from Dallas ... Saudi clients.

Oil meetings.

"I couldn't, Kevin. I was never one hundred percent certain they had taken Sarah or that they had her. I couldn't have spoken out against a client without proof. The wealth of these people ... do you know what they are capable of?"

I look up. They are both now standing, squaring off from each other. Kevin's hands are clenched into fists beside his body, knuckles whitening. Gone are the earlier tears of relief. All I can see in his expression is anger and betrayal, reminiscent of our last argument.

Kevin sneers before yelling his response. "Well, they stole my daughter, so I have a fair idea of what they're capable of."

"I'm sorry, Kevin. But you know I'd never—" she whispers, bringing her hand up to cup his face, only to have him slap it away.

"Don't!" Kevin takes a step back and shakes his head. His body is trembling, and we're drawing attention from people in the foyer. "I can't believe you never said anything. You *knew* how I grieved for her. Fuck! Jacquie, you listened to my confessions, hoping she was dead—

because death would be so much better than a life of prostitution or slavery. Damn you, Jacquie."

"I'm sorry! I-I had my suspicions, but I never knew, okay?" She collapses into the chair and closes her eyes. "I never knew," she repeats as a whisper.

I blink at the revelations and add them to my own. It all makes sense now—why the Dubai Police never made any additional arrests other than the Filipino woman and the supposed Russian mobster.

Why the investigation was closed.

Why nothing was ever uncovered.

"Oh my God!" I finally speak out loud. "I can't believe you never said anything. Screw your attorney-client privileges. Where's your morality? Where's your ..." I stop, close my eyes, and gather my thoughts.

This bitch has single-handedly taken a wrecking ball to my marriage, my family, my life.

When I open my eyes, I see her blurred form through tear-soaked eyes. I scrub my face with my hands before gathering the photos and replacing them in the envelope.

Standing, I take a moment to study the woman I once considered somewhat of a friend. One who betrayed me by having an affair with my husband. That betrayal seems pitiful compared to the one now unraveling before us. We can't go back and change our pasts. We have to live with those decisions forever. I hope she rots in hell for all of her past transgressions. I doubt this one—as monumental as it is—is the only one she has hidden away. But, for what it's worth, I am done.

"This is something you'll need to live with for the rest of your life. I feel sorry for you."

With a shake of my head, I turn and walk away. I need to cool off before Kevin and I meet up with Sarah.

37

———

I'm sitting on the other side of the lobby in Rosewood Hotel's aptly named Living Room, recounting in my mind the last ten years and fuming over Jacquie's role in it all when Kevin finds me. I saw him on my return, seated with his head in his hands, clearly deep in thought, the contents of the envelope scattered on the coffee table in front of him. I gave him space.

Jacquie's absence is a telling sign that their conversation didn't end well. For me, the realization that she had an idea of Sarah's location all these years is devastating. Time spent hoping and praying Sarah was alive and hadn't been sold into slavery or prostitution ... and Jacquie knew where she was. The lost years could have been cut in half if she'd had the decency to speak up.

"Do you know where we're meeting them?" With his shoulders hunched and eyes full of sadness and regret, Kevin's words are flat and lacking expression.

I'm about to answer when I see a familiar face behind him.

"Our FBI contact is here. He'll tell us where we need to be." I point to Special Agent Brody, who's walking toward us.

Kevin nods once, his Adam's apple bobbing as a single tear rolls down his face. He swiftly wipes it away and regains his composure before the agent reaches us.

Brody keeps the introductions brief, and we're quickly led to an elevator. Too caught up in my family saga, I didn't notice the increased security in the hotel. It might not be obvious to the ordinary person, but as Special Agent Brody escorts us, a look passes between him and more than one hotel bystander.

During the elevator's ascent, Brody briefs us on the schedule of events the Saudis have agreed to.

Nayef al-Tuhar is allowing us to meet Sarah alone in a suite as a sign of good faith. Kevin scoffs at this, but I understand. Sarah's twenty-one and the wife to al-Tuhar's son. As a woman in their culture and a member of the al-Tuhar family, she'd normally be escorted by a male member of the family. Allowing us to see her alone shows a trust that makes me hopeful.

We're led to a door on the top floor and told to enter and wait. The door shuts behind us with a soft click, and I jump at the noise before silently scolding myself. The suite is opulent and contains its own sitting room. I sit, and Kevin comes to a halt before the window, keeping his back to me.

"I'm sorry," he says, his voice cracking on the words, as he stares at the view of our national Capitol.

His words spark a flourish of anger within me that contrasts the rolling of my stomach. I close my eyes and swallow. It's not the time for arguments. I understand why he voiced his apologies, but whatever his guilt, whatever the crimes he's punishing himself for, in this moment, it's none of my concern.

I close my eyes and take a deep breath.

What if, regardless of the DNA results, this isn't Sarah? What if the results were a false positive, and this is all a cruel joke? These and many other questions crash through my head.

We've never come this close to finding her. *What if it's all a mistake?*

I cross my legs and squeeze them together to alleviate the twitchiness of my muscles. Finding no relief, I stand and join Kevin at the window. He stands statuesque with a stiff smile, caught up in his own thoughts and memories.

The click of a closing door has us both startling, and we turn in unison to see a beautiful young woman wearing a silken blue skirt and blouse. She drops her headscarf to her shoulders, unveiling shoulder-length blonde hair. With hesitant steps, she moves toward us, mouth curving up to a smile.

"Mother? Father?" The melodic words have an accent that has come from years of not speaking English.

"Sarah?" I'm moving before I can stop myself, and I pull her into an embrace.

Arms envelop me from behind as Kevin joins in. "Sarah …"

EPILOGUE

I don't believe in the myths and stories of Arabia. They're just stories created by overactive imaginations, trying to glamorize something that was once an unknown. Aladdin, Ali Baba, and Sinbad the Sailor do not and never did exist. The *Alf laylah wa laylah*, or *The Arabian Nights*, are no more than a collection of stories from the Middle East and India, dating back to the Islamic Golden Age and compiled over many hundreds of years by people looking for a way to escape their dreary lives.

There is no magic lamp or a magic doorway. Nor can you camp on a sleeping whale or converse with dwarves or one-eyed giants. These stories were created to tell a tale of good versus bad, rich versus poor, and to provide hope for the down-and-out for something more.

But the desert rose? How can a rose survive the desert? The rose with its symbol for promise, hope, and new beginnings. The symbol for love. Is it because of what it represents that it overcomes the harshness of the desert?

One legend tells the tale of the most beautiful rose with the most mesmerizing aroma that could only be found within the desert. It's said that this desert rose exists as a sign of God, or Allah, for all those who are lost and suffering exhaustion with lack of food and water—a promise to find strength during the difficult moments and to always search out the beauty. The desert rose is a symbol of love and the purity of love.

The desert rose is a misnomer because it's not a rose. It's a succulent known as the adenium obesum, and it thrives in the harshest of environments. It's a slow grower, and whether it's planted from a cutting or from seed, it might take months or years until it blooms. It needs sunlight to grow and sunlight to flower.

In so many ways, I can see why Sarah was dubbed the desert rose. Why she has become the desert rose.

In an abandoned and empty space such as the desert, the rose represents power. It shows how something so small and possibly overlooked can hold such strength. With all the elements working against it, it can somehow forgo water and thrive with the constant heat and perpetual sun. Despite its trials, it continues to grow, bringing hope because what is the chance a bee or insect can happen upon it for germination? What is the chance a bird or a traveler would carry the seed in the first place? What is the chance another traveler might pass to admire the lonely rose? For how can beauty grow in such a vast, empty place? What does this rose really represent?

What's forgotten about the traditional rose are the thorns that hide beneath the beauty. Hidden underneath the green foliage below the silken texture of the petals, the thorns act as the flower's defense and symbolize loss. They will prick you in its act of protector if you try to pluck them away.

If Sarah is the rose, I am the thorns.

How can I refute that the Arabian tales are all but lies? How can I?

Maybe they're not lies. But I don't want to believe it.

I don't.

But, for Sarah, I will try. Because, if she is the rose, then I am the thorns. So, I will try.

ACKNOWLEDGMENTS

Writing a book is like raising a child. It starts as an idea and is followed by periods of time while it stumbles and falls and desperately tries to find its voice. As the author, there's the constant concern and worry, wondering if you're doing the right thing. Giving it the right voice, the right representation, until it's done and it's time to send it out into the big, bad world to succeed or fail on its own merits. A child isn't raised by one person alone, nor is a book written in isolation.

The idea for *Desert Rose* came about many years ago as I lived an expat life in Dubai. I was drinking coffee with a group of moms after dropping the kids off at school, listening to one of them retell her experience at Carrefour the evening before. She had lost her daughter in the aisles. She said she was frantic, yelling and running up and down the aisles in the store, searching for her. Her daughter had wandered off and was being led to the security desk by a South Asian couple when the mother finally found her. That one story sparked an idea, questioning what would've happened if she'd been abducted. How would such an incident play out within a culturally rich and diverse environment? Also, who would abduct a pretty little girl and for what reason? But I suppose most intriguing would be how something like this would affect the mother and the family dynamics, given where this incident occurred. So, what resulted is Jen's story. Her journey is fiction, closely interwoven with varying truths.

It should be noted here that Dubai offered the perfect backdrop for this story. It's a wonderful city, and it was a great place to live and bring up children. It's safe, and it offers so many opportunities for young families. Dubai is a melting pot of cultural diversity and embraces all people and religions. Where else would you be able to visit Santa while the call to prayer sounds? The expat community is close-knit, and some of my most trusted friends were forged while living there. There are three women who make up the character Melanie—Melanie, Monica, and Kylie. Our friendship spans cultures and continents, and I am thankful every day to have met them.

My husband remains my biggest cheerleader, my confidant, and my alpha reader. He patiently listened to me read chapters aloud as the snow fell silently outside the kitchen window. He'd debate and brainstorm scenarios with me and try not to get too frustrated when I reminded him that this story was not an academic piece of writing but a work of fiction.

Tarryn Fisher and her author group gave me the confidence and the tools to write. Through her, I was able to connect with other authors and share their journeys. She introduced me to my wonderful beta readers—Sandra Damien, T.L. Fisher, Heather Bentley, and Bre Lockhart. Reading their thoughts and comments was truly humbling.

Jessica Gibson, my alpha reader and coach, was the one who kept me accountable by messaging me every day to make sure I was writing and then reading the nonsense on a weekly basis. Knowing I had to answer her messages made me get behind the computer and actually write.

Sandra Dee is my unicorn. I honestly don't know what I bring to our friendship, but I'm so happy to have connected with her through Tarryn Fisher's online group. She patiently answers all of my stupid questions and listens to my ridiculous rants. She's my book bestie, and I love hanging out and drinking with her—although we don't get to do that often, as she lives in Vancouver while I'm in Alaska. Thank goodness Tarryn organizes retreats and conferences for us to meet up.

If you've made it this far, thank you.

I love to read; it's one of my many favorite things. By taking the time to get to this point, we have so much in common.

If you liked this book (or even if you didn't), please consider leaving a review. You might not think it makes a difference, but it does. Reviews—good, bad, or otherwise—tell other people that an author is worth reading. And, as an indie author, it's one way to help get our name out there.

Thank you.

READING GROUP GUIDE

Discussion Questions for *Desert Rose*

1. What three words or phrases best describe the *Desert Rose?*

2. What character did you most relate to and why?

3. Do you think Jen's ability to get answers was limited because of her gender? If so, how?

4. How did Kevin's actions after the kidnapping make you feel about him? How do you think the outcome would have changed had his actions been different?

5. Which, if any, supporting characters did you feel either a strong appreciation or dislike for?

6. What scene or moment made you connect with story?

7. How would this story differ if the kidnapping had taken place in the US?

8. Name the one main emotion you felt after finishing *Desert Rose*.

9. *Desert Rose* ends with a sense of closure. Did you find the ending to have equal compensation for the years of distrust and grief? Can happy endings assuage the overwhelming feeling of loss?

10. You are the casting director for the film adaptation. What actors are you choosing for each character?

ABOUT THE AUTHOR

K. Moore is an Australian braving the subzero Alaskan temperatures with her husband and two sons while battling agitated moose, nosy brown bears, and a Karelian bear dog named Hathor. She's an avid reader, hiker, and CrossFit enthusiast. If you manage to locate a decent bottle of gin and a chair at the bar, she might be convinced to regale you with tales of her global travels. Without the gin, you'll have to find the evidence within the pages of her stories and poetry.

Find K. Moore online at:

www.AuthorKMoore.com

www.facebook.com/AuthorKMoore

Instagram and Twitter: @runs2ny

Keep up-to-date and sign up for K. Moore's newsletter:

http://bit.ly/kmoorenews

www.ingramcontent.com/pod-product-compliance
Lightning Source LLC
Chambersburg PA
CBHW050240110726
47898CB00007B/2218